Misfits in
the Kingdom

Garner Fritts

Chapter One

"**I** have you now!"

My horse galloped furiously toward the vicious animal. It rounded the tree in full stride, spun around, and flung leaves and dirt into the air. The monster grunted and snorted at me. I pulled hard on my reins and brought my steed to a full stop. The hounds slid forward as they came to a halt behind me. They barked loudly at the creature. My men were on horseback. They circled the beast on each side and waited. I held up my hand and signaled for them to hold their position.

"Steady…steady…" I tossed my lasso around the thick neck of the feisty boar. I leaned backward and pulled the rope tight. The beast thrashed its head around and squealed like a crazed animal.

"Lord Adrian, be careful that you…" one of my knights beckoned.

It was too late. The boar darted into the woods with the noose securely around its neck. It jerked me off of my mare and slammed me into the ground. I knew the safest thing to do would be to let go of the rope and hope that my men could catch the animal. Yet I had to prove myself to my soldiers. I gripped the lasso tighter. The beast ran hard and dragged me through the forest.

"Let go my lord!" a knight called to me from behind.

"We will come and assist you!" another knight said.

"Hold your positions!" I commanded. "I will conquer this beast yet!"

Leaves flew in all directions, briars pricked my sides, and small sticks jabbed me repeatedly as I tried to pull myself closer to the large boar. My shoulders burned from the strain of holding the rope for so long, and my hands stung with the pain of the lasso burrowing tight against my palms. If I gave up now, I would lose my honor in front of the men. I had to keep fighting. I pulled myself higher off the ground and closer to the boar. It continued to charge ahead in full fury. My forearms and chest no longer dragged against the ground; my knees scraped against the forest floor. All the pain would be worth taking down this violent beast and hearing praises from my knights.

"Look out my lord!" one of the men cried.

I turned to see which of my knights called to me. Some of them pointed directly ahead while the rest yelled their concerns. I turned to look in the direction they pointed. A brown blur slammed into my chest and knocked the wind out of me. The blow was so hard; I lost my grip on the rope. It slid out of my hands and left burning welts. My vision blurred, but I managed to glance downward and see what hit me.

I was sprawled across a jagged tree stump, unable to move or catch my breath.

"The beast is turning to attack!" someone said.

The boar stood a full stadia from where I was. It crouched down and scraped its hooves against the ground. I saw the rage in its eyes even from this distance. It meant to charge into me and end my life. The animal lunged toward me as fast as its powerful legs would carry it. I couldn't move. I tried calling for the aid of my knights, but no sound came from my throat. I waved my hand toward the creature in a feeble motion, trying to deter it from charging. It didn't work.

A knight shot out of the bushes on horseback and hoisted a javelin at the pig. It squealed and slumped to the ground as the point of the spear sank into its head. The hounds surrounded me and licked my face. I pushed them away and tried to stand up. Two of the knights ran up and helped me to my feet while the other six men saluted my masked savior.

"Are you well my lord?" one of them asked.

I rubbed my ribs. "I'm fine." I felt sore all over, but nothing seemed to be broken. I stumbled over to the heroic knight who rescued me. "Who are you sir that I might reward your bravery?"

The mystery knight dismounted and stood before me. He was decked out in silver chain mail and wore the emblem of Granes on his mail shirt underneath. It was the symbol of my father and my family. The stranger pulled his helmet off of his head.

"Sir Marcus!" the other knights exclaimed.

It was my chief knight. His long brown braided

hair hung across each side of his muscled shoulders. A light beard shadowed his face. He knelt before me on one knee. "It is good that I subdued the boar in time. It would pain me to see my lord turned to fodder." He stood up and straightened his glove. "Are you well Lord Adrian?"

I wiped the blood from my split lip. "I nearly had the beast until it used his cunning. The creature had the strength of ten bears." It wasn't that strong. I was trying to keep from being totally humiliated. "You were lucky to have taken it by surprise."

"Of course my lord," Marcus replied. "Shall we take the boar home for supper?"

I nodded and shrugged off any hands that tried to assist me. My honor was wounded worse than my body.

We journeyed in silence back to my county. Two of my knights held a long pole between their horses. The dead boar dangled by its hooves where they had tied it to the pole. It was as if my men sensed my frustration.

"Open the gates," I commanded.

Granes was one of seven counties in the province of Elos. It was the smallest in comparison to other castles and manors, but it was rich in goods and well protected by dense forests and thick stone walls. The gates hummed as they lifted upward. I entered on my magnificent steed followed by Sir Marcus and the eight soldiers.

My beloved wife emerged from the manor and came to meet us. Wensla wore a bronze colored dress. Her attire and her wavy hair swayed in the gentle breeze that whisked through the yard. She smiled at me with those ruby red lips I loved so much. She was as beautiful as the first time I had met her three years prior. Wensla ran to me with her arms outstretched.

"Adrian are you well?" she asked.

"I'm a bit bruised but fine otherwise." I pointed to the boar that the knights carried. "I was attacked by this vicious beast."

The soldiers rode beyond us toward the stables. They nodded to me as each one passed. Wensla motioned for the manor servants, and they fetched a damp cloth for her.

Marcus dismounted, placed his hand on my shoulder, and looked to Wensla. "My lady, I wanted you to know that I am so glad that I was there to…"

"I weakened the boar and Sir Marcus finished him off," I interrupted. I wasn't about to let him take all the glory. I was the lord of this manor, not him.

"It is as my lord speaks my lady," Marcus said to Wensla.

"The children tell me you have been sharing your story again of how you saved the kingdom." Wensla patted my cut lip with a damp cloth. "I would think my lord would have more things to do than play story-teller to the children of Granes." She straightened my cloak and brushed leaves off of the sleeve of my tunic.

I took the rag from her and held it to my wound. "I am only doing as my lady does. Were you not telling the maidens the other day of how you rescued me as you played the part of an angel?"

Wensla rolled her eyes. "I only did so because the young women in Granes asked me how you and

I fell in love."

Something was happening between Wensla and me. The first years of our marriage were as heaven on earth. We took moonlit walks through the yard and gazed into the twinkling stars for a long time. We talked frequently about our hopes and dreams. We wrestled one another in the stables and rolled through the hay laughing. We did none of this now. She busied herself organizing the manor while I made sport with the men and travelled the countryside. Wensla's father Vigilan knew nothing of our troubles. Neither of us spoke about it.

. Marcus threw a bag at Wensla's feet that jingled when it hit the ground. "A gift for my lady." He bowed before her.

"A gracious gift from my husband's greatest knight," Wensla said. She smiled and nodded in acknowledgement.

Did Wensla have feelings for Sir Marcus? He was quite handsome and very arrogant. He and I were the same age – nineteen. Whereas I had been a late bloomer to knighthood, Marcus was dubbed a knight by the king at the age of fifteen. I acquired my knighthood through one act of divine opportunity; Marcus gained his status through training and many hard fought battles. No one was quite the swordsman that my chief knight was. He and I sparred often. Marcus never openly expressed it, but I sensed that he felt superior to me. He always stopped short of bringing me down during swordplay, and then he would salute the townspeople who gathered to watch.

My chest burned and my face flushed with anger.

I breathed deeply so as not to show my jealousy. After all, Marcus had never opposed me openly. If I were to be presumptuous in my judgments, I would lose my noble dignity in the sight of the people of Granes. It was a mistake I could ill afford to make.

"What is in the bag?" I asked.

Marcus turned to me and did obeisance. "Pardon, my lord. I did not address this matter with you first." He pointed to the bag. "I brought gold and precious jewels from the hands of thieves." He slashed his sword through the air. "We encountered twenty of them before meeting you for the hunt, but they were no match for me and my men."

"I saw no prisoners among us," I said. "Why did you not capture them?"

"They refused to be taken," Marcus replied. "They left us no choice. We had to cut them down so none of them could escape." He rubbed his fuzzy chin. "We left their dead carcasses to rot neath the trees. They will make a great feast for some wild animals." Marcus turned to Wensla and sighed. "Unfortunately this is sometimes necessary, but I will endeavor to be more chivalrous in my future encounters."

"Do you know where they obtained their loot?" I asked.

Marcus shook his head. "I suppose these thieves were greedy town folk looking to make a name for themselves. I heard rumors that they plundered and killed many who journeyed through the forest. People feared to travel those roads." Marcus pointed to me. "They breathed threats against your kingdom my lord." Marcus grabbed the bag of booty, untied it and held gold coins for all to see. "The soldiers have more treasures to present you with. We have wrought a great victory today for God and Granes."

"You shall be handsomely rewarded for such bravery," Wensla said. She clasped my arm. "I must prepare a feast for all my weary soldiers. This boar will make a special treat for all."

I nodded in acknowledgement. As I watched Wensla walk away, I wondered if she desired this heroic knight in my service. When I was a lad, I heard tales of how Queen Guinevere fell in love with Sir Lancelot while he was in the service of King Arthur, and how the pair ran away together. I wished to warn Sir Marcus, but I felt that chivalry should still prevent me from unproven accusations.

Marcus handed the bag of loot to one of my attendants and moved closer to me. He looked both ways and then leaned near my ear. "There is another urgent matter my lord."

We moved beyond all of the servants. I looked both ways to make sure no one was nearby. "Say on."

"Before our encounter with the thieves and the boar, I met a monk travelling from the Dayma monastery to bring you news. I told him that I would relay the message and he could be on his way."

"What was the message?" I asked.

"Trouble is brewing in the church, and the abbot of Dayma wishes to speak with you concerning the matter. I was asked to repeat this message only to you in private. He requests that you do not delay."

It had been months since I had seen Eli or the beloved monastery. What could be happening? My dear friend had never bidden me to come there. I motioned to Marcus.

"Prepare my horse. I ride to Dayma."

Chapter Two

⊗⊗⊗

I alighted from my horse and approached the massive door of the Dayma monastery. The first time I came to this holy place, it felt like a dungeon. It eventually became a sacred haven where I met my closest friend, declared my love for Wensla, and learned the fear of God. Dayma was special. I shook myself from my daydream and looked over my shoulder. My two servants dismounted from their horses and joined me. I grabbed the knocker and pounded it against the heavy wooden door. Each strike made a loud thud. The door drummed open and the bulgy eyed porter peeped his head out.

"Lord Adrian, it is good to see you!" the monk said.

"Yes," I replied. "Tell the abbot that the Baron of Granes is here to see him."

A smile broke across the monk's face. He waved us inside. "Come, come. Abbot Eli is expecting you."

We followed this small man toward the abbot's quarters. As I looked around the monastery grounds, many images flashed in my mind from three years prior. It seemed like a dream from long ago. The monk led us down the pathway past beautiful gardens to the familiar hallway with arched ceilings.

I pointed toward the nearby buildings. "Would you mind to take my servants to the stables?"

The bulgy eyed monk nodded. "As you say my lord."

I motioned to the two attendants. "Go to the stables and wait for me there."

The servants nodded and followed the bulgy eyed monk. A thin figure moved from the shadows in the hallway. The gray eyes of Eli met mine, and he smiled with his sheepish grin. He embraced me with a hug.

"My dear friend," he said. "It has been too long. How are you faring? How is Wensla?"

"We are well and Granes is prospering. We had a good harvest recently." I moved closer to him. "Sir Marcus told me that you bear news of trouble in the church."

Eli bade me to join him at a nearby table. We sat down in high back wooden chairs on opposite sides. Eli looked both ways and leaned forward. "Pope Regent XII is dying Adrian," he whispered. "Two prominent archbishops seek to replace him. It is the decision of Regent to appoint a successor, for he speaks on behalf of God."

"Who is being considered to stand in his stead?"

We heard movement outside, so we sat silently until the commotion faded into the distance. Eli cleared his throat and again leaned forward.

"Leo, archbishop of Maltivia, is the first under consideration. The other is Darian, an archbishop who already resides in The City. Darian assists Regent in many matters because of the pope's failing strength."

I knew Archbishop Leo. He was a calm, peaceful man who beheld visions from the Lord. He visited Granes over a year ago to bless the larger chapel I had built for my townspeople. I felt warmth and peace in his presence. Even though I had deep reverence for Leo, many in the church considered him to be insane and weak. I heard he was highly respected in his home of Maltivia. Although it was a town of merchants and business, it was said to be spiritually prosperous under the guidance of its beloved archbishop. With such a powerful and zealous leader as Darian aiding Regent, why would Leo be considered for the position? Rumor was Darian held sway over many powerful kings and rulers, and that his presence made men tremble. He was a symbol of strength and religious fervor. There had to be more to this controversy. Perhaps Eli could shed light on this mysterious situation.

"You probably wonder why Leo is considered if Darian is such a good candidate," Eli whispered.

It was as if he read my thoughts as in times past. I nodded.

"Everyone in Christendom is wondering the same thing," Eli said. "The rumor is that Regent suspects the motives and desires of his right hand archbishop. I heard that he prays constantly about his pending death and his successor. Although Darian has never been known to betray the pope, Regent hesitates to appoint him. It is said that Leo of Maltivia is a name whispered often in Regent's heart. No one would dare openly question the pope's authority on this matter, but many are secretly wondering if Regent has gone mad."

I felt the same way the pope did. Just as he was uncertain he could trust his right hand advisor, I wasn't so sure I could trust my chief knight. Perhaps I needed to pray as much as Regent, then God would lead me to a similar answer.

"What is our role in this matter?" I asked.

Eli pulled a letter from his cloak and opened it. "Pope Regent XII summons all from far and near to come to The City in preparation for deciding the next reigning pope. All lords, kings, barons, dukes, princes, abbots, priests, cardinals, archbishops, and bishops are to be in attendance. We are to appear before him in the outer courtyard three days from now." Eli lowered the letter and stared intently at me. "The messenger who delivered this to me was a personal attendant of Regent. He told me that the pope has extended a special invitation to Eli of Dayma and Adrian of Granes, for he respects our thoughts above all others."

I felt a lump in my throat. Pope Regent, leader of all Christendom, called me and my friend by name? Why would someone so great think so highly of us? There were many rulers and religious leaders more prominent than the both of us. Perhaps Eli had heard wrong. The letter in the hand of my dear friend was quite real. I stood to my feet.

"I must prepare for our journey. Will you be accompanying our band?"

Eli stood up and nodded. "I will be with you. Lord Vigilan will also be joining us."

"Very well then," I replied. "I will see you tomorrow."

I rode back to Granes in silence. I searched my thoughts over and over. Why would the pope summon me by name? The stories of my bravery against the Tartars must have reached his ears. Many men in the kingdom had done acts of chivalry. Why would I be singled out among them? There had to be another reason. When we reached Granes, I made my way to the yard where my knights were practicing swordplay. Sir Marcus demonstrated to the onlookers how to thrust the enemy quickly with a sword not yet drawn. They gasped with delight at how speedily he unsheathed his weapon. As I approached, they ceased their games and turned to look at me.

"What is it lord?" Marcus asked.

"Get the men ready. We leave by morning to journey to The City. Bring whatever provisions are necessary."

Sir Marcus bowed. "As you wish my lord." He clapped his hands together in the direction of the soldiers. "Make haste to prepare an escort for Lord Adrian tomorrow." The soldiers scattered in every direction as Marcus barked orders. He looked at me and saluted. "We shall be ready." He walked away toward the stables.

I ventured into the refectory where Wensla directed her maids in cleaning up the kitchen. She waved to me. I motioned for her with my finger and she followed me just outside the doorway. Wensla stood there with arms folded and waited for me to speak. In times past, she would have embraced me and kissed me on the lips. I swallowed hard and bit my lip. I was determined not to let her know I was troubled by her actions. I wasn't sure if I was feeling jealous of Marcus, bothered by her lack of affection toward me, concerned over the news of the church election, or troubled over all three. I would only mention the latter.

"What ails you husband?"

I took her by the hand and walked in silence. We went into the castle, through the hallway, up the stairs, and into our chambers. Wensla sat on the edge of the bed and stared at me. I closed the door behind us, walked over to my wife, folded my arms in the same manner as she had done, and sighed deeply. She stared at me with a blank expression and awaited my news. She didn't seem to be disturbed by my cold demeanor.

"There is controversy in Christendom." I would not reveal my feelings about Sir Marcus or her lack of respect. It was not the proper time.

"What grim news do you have?"

"During my visit with Eli, I learned that our blessed pope is dying, and that he is seeking to elect a new pope." I paused and rubbed the back of my neck. "Pope Regent XII has given a special invitation to me and Eli."

Wensla stood to her feet and wrinkled her brow. "The pope has personally summoned you?"

"All rulers and orders have been summoned to The City for a grand meeting in the matter," I replied. "We are to appear before his holiness in three days. I will be travelling with your father and Eli tomorrow."

I turned toward the door. "Sir Marcus and the

knights will be accompanying me. I will leave some foot soldiers behind to guard the county." Perhaps I was reacting as a child, but I did not want to see her reaction to my mentioning of Sir Marcus. I did not want to look at her at all because she had treated me so disrespectfully.

"Very well then."

Wensla's voice was devoid of any feeling. She didn't seem to care about what I told her. She gave me a quick peck on the cheek, opened the door, walked down the corridor, and made her way down the stairs. Her wavy light brown hair bounced with each step she took.

I did not understand what was happening between us, but I had more important matters to attend to at the moment. Why did the pope call this election? Why did he not trust his right hand advisor? Why had he summoned me by special invitation? I would find my answer in what would probably become a heated debate.

Chapter Three

The sun peeked over the horizon casting a yellow glow on the fields. A light, warm breeze swirled around us. Lord Vigilan's steed was on my left hand and Eli's mule was on my right hand. Sir Marcus and the other knights from Granes followed close behind with some monks from the Dayma monastery. Vigilan's knights from Tiempo followed them. My father-in-law's chief knight had remained behind to guard his manor. I counted seventeen men in our band.

"How is my daughter faring?" Vigilan asked.

"She is well," I replied. I looked out of the corner of my eye to see if Sir Marcus would react to the name of my beloved. Marcus looked ahead with a blank stare.

"Eli tells me a special invitation has been granted to you," Vigilan said. "Have you ever been to The City?"

I shook my head. "This is my first visit."

"It is a magnificent place," Eli said. "I have been there on several pilgrimages. The buildings and much of the streets are lined with gold. It as if one is visiting Heaven on earth."

"Do you have any other news of this church dispute?" I asked Vigilan.

The lord of Tiempo shook his head. "Nothing more than what you know already. It is strange that his holiness would request the presence of those other than the clergy to procure advice on such a serious matter."

I didn't answer Vigilan. I wondered the same thing myself. Our band of travellers rode steadily along the pathway leading to The City. We met many groups going to the same destination for the same purpose. Some were great rulers and knights with caravans much larger than ours. We set up campfires and tents by night along the way, and then moved forward once again by the light of dawn. By the third day, we passed ruined buildings on each side of the road and joined a large group of masses who moved slowly toward The City. Commotion filled the air.

Eli pointed into the faint distance. "There it is."

I squinted and saw something gleaming like a shiny mirror. As we moved closer, the glowing light grew brighter. Tall buildings made of marble towered above us on each side. These structures were the largest I had ever seen. They paled any castle by comparison. The stone pavement beneath our horses transformed into glistening gold. The glory and magnificence of this place overwhelmed me. Stable keepers helped us off our horses and led them away. We walked toward a massive open square where a large golden balcony shimmered in the sunlight above us.

"This is the Court of Declaration," Eli said. "Nobles and churchmen come here to receive instruction or other proclamations from his holiness."

I heard whispers around me as all eyes turned toward the balcony. Everyone seemed to hold their breath in anticipation of who might appear from the scene above. We followed the clergy and nobility up the marble stairs into a giant hallway with the largest arched ceilings I had ever seen. Numerous lords, clergymen, and knights stood on each side at rows of tables. Our posse went to a specific area as the attendants directed.

"This is the Debate Hall," Eli whispered into my ear.

Golden steps led to a large golden throne on the far end of the hall. Two smaller thrones stood on each side of the larger seat. A man with stringy gray hair, many wrinkles, deep blue eyes, and a slight smile sat on the left hand throne. It was Archbishop Leo. A purple robed man with dark silvery hair, a hooked nose, pointy chin, and black pupils sat on the right hand side.

"Who is the one on the right?" I asked Vigilan. I was sure I already knew.

Vigilan looked down at the table and stroked his beard. "That is Archbishop Darian. Almost everyone in Christendom fears his divine authority."

I understood why. This clerical figure sent chills through me. Darian rose to his feet and clapped his hands together several times. The hall grew quiet.

"Honored guests." Darian's voice rumbled

through the hall. It was deep and powerful. "His holiness, Pope Regent XII, comes."

Everyone in the hall rose to their feet and lowered their head in reverence. A tall slender figure appeared from a side room assisted by monks. Regent was humped over and leaned on a staff. He reminded me of a withering tree. Regent's golden robes sparkled as beams of sunlight shined on it through a nearby window. He slowly ascended the steps and extended his hand to the waiting archbishops. Darian kissed the ring on his finger, and then Leo did the same. Regent slowly made his way to his seat and everyone sat down.

"My children," Regent said. He spoke with a raspy voice. "I have summoned you before God and His saints because I do not have much longer to live here on this earth." He placed a clenched fist toward his mouth and coughed. "I have been troubled by these thoughts, and I have prayed for guidance from the Holy Ghost and from the writings of the holy fathers. I was compelled to call this assembly and seek out its council."

"If you wish to be recognized," Darian said, "rise slowly and sign the cross."

An earl with curly blonde hair, brown eyes, and tanned skin stood up and signed the cross.

Darian nodded.

"With all due respect your holiness, I believe God has shown you the obvious choice." The fair haired man held his hand out. "Although Archbishop Leo is a just and good man, Archbishop Darian wields the spiritual fervor of the Lion of Judah. This is necessary to lead souls in God's kingdom."

Whispers and nods of agreement filled the room. Darian folded both hands together as if he was praying and a smile broke across his face. Leo closed his eyes and sighed. Pope Regent rubbed his chin as if pondering the idea. For the next few hours, rulers of kingdoms and church clergy gave testimony in favor of Archbishop Darian. No one spoke on behalf of Leo. The reasons were the same, just spoken with different words. My chest burned with anger. Something about Darian didn't seem right. How could I let my long-time friend be slandered? I could stand it no longer.

"It is divine leading that… "

. "I speak for Archbishop Leo!" I stood to my feet and pounded the table with my palms.

The fat cardinal who spoke stopped and stared at me with widened eyes. Everyone looked at me and whispers filled the room. Darian rose to his feet and pointed at me.

"Young man," he thundered, "you were not recognized properly. You have disgraced his holiness and insulted this assembly. Sit down and be silent!"

Pope Regent held up his hand in protest. "Wait!" he said. He leaned forward in his chair. "Who are you my son?"

"I am Lord Adrian of Granes," I said. "I meant no irreverence your holiness. We have heard why Archbishop Darian should be the next pope. I would give you reasons why Archbishop Leo should be your divine successor." I felt a churning in my stomach. Who was I to advise such powerful and holy men?

"Are you not the Adrian who saved all of

Christendom nearly three years ago from the Tartars?" Regent asked.

I nodded and my face flushed. It was one thing to recount my stories before small children; it was quite another to speak of it during such an important meeting. It was as if all thoughts emptied from my mind. For a brief moment, my mouth opened but no sounds came out.

Vigilan tugged on my tunic. "Ask for pardon and take your seat!" he whispered.

Regent smiled and coughed again. "I have heard of your devotion to God and His kingdom. I would be most curious to know why you feel such things in your heart."

Darian slowly sat down into his seat and watched me closely. Out of the corner of my eye, I saw Eli bowing his head and praying. The hall grew silent.

"Archbishop Leo is a man of faith with the humility of the Christ. Those from his dwelling in Maltivia will attest to his righteous ways. Even many in this assembly have already spoken on behalf of his holy character. He visited my county to administer blessings, and we have prospered since. Everywhere the archbishop turns, men are blessed."

"I will agree to that," Eli said as he rose to his feet.

"And you are…?" Regent asked.

"I…I am…Abbot Eli of Dayma," Eli stuttered. His face flushed and he looked downward. The intimidation of the moment was evident in my friend. "I know of many priests from Maltivia who will speak of the holy influence of Archbishop Leo." He kept his head down as he spoke.

"Such disrespect to your eminence," Darian snorted. He turned to Regent. "This assembly is getting out of hand. They disregard God and divine order."

Regent recognized the Baron of Sansaat, and he stood to speak. The man had a red shaggy beard and emerald green eyes. He stretched out his hands toward everyone in the hall. "Shall we adhere to the words of a boy whose own chief knight bests him in combat? A child who never fought an actual battle for the glory of the church? And shall we listen to the words of a sickly monk whose speech is but babble?"

The hall roared with laughter. Eli and I sunk into our chairs. I felt as if I had lost a duel.

Regent held up his hand to silence the scoffers. "I will give all these things great consideration. Although I have heard many strong arguments for Darian, the friends of Archbishop Leo have given merit to his cause." He slowly rose to his feet, and the hall rose after him. "My decision will be made in the coming weeks."

I sprang from my seat after Darian dismissed the assembly. Eli, Vigilan, and those of our fellowship departed quickly from the hall. We spoke to no one and darted through the crowds. A baron with a falcon on his arm watched me and whispered something to another baron. Both of them looked at me and laughed. Others shouted at me, calling me a blasphemer and an ignorant child. Some stammered and made sport of Eli. I was amazed at the ridicule from such godly figures and chivalric rulers. Perhaps this is what the pope recognized as well. No matter what rank they held, I refused to allow their scorn to trouble me. I hardened my face like a proud warrior. I would not let them know I was troubled by their taunts.

After our fellowship traveled far away from The City, Sir Marcus brought his horse next to mine. "My lord, we will make every effort to protect you. I heard threats made against your life."

"I can fend for myself!" I snapped.

Sir Marcus looked surprised at my response. The words of the Baron of Sansaat played in my mind over and over. I had denied it before, but it was evident that I was jealous of my chief knight.

"My apologies," I said to Marcus. "I am distressed in these matters."

"I understand my lord," Marcus replied. "I seek only your welfare." He pulled on his reins and fell back behind me.

"You and Eli have aroused the wrath of many throughout the land," Vigilan said. "I fear for your safety too. That is why I beckoned you to recant. For some unknown reason, you and the Abbot of Dayma have a strong voice with the pope. Others see this and are quite displeased. Be on guard my son. If you need my hand or that of my knights, send for me and I will come to your aid without delay."

"God will protect us," Eli said. He signed the cross.

I nodded to Vigilan's offer and Eli's words but said nothing. I parted ways with my allies and made my way back to Granes. Was there danger ahead for me or my dear friend? The coming days would reveal that answer.

Chapter Four

Wensla closed her eyes and sighed when I told her the grim news of the meeting in The City. I didn't know if she even cared or was too troubled to speak. No matter my fate, I wanted to find a way to reconcile to my wife. Two weeks passed. I heard no news from Dayma, Tiempo, The City, or anywhere else. I sent my knights to scout for enemies and bring me word of any plots or schemes against my life. There was nothing. I dreaded not knowing what would befall me. One afternoon, a messenger burst through the door.

"My lord, someone approaches the gates of Granes!" The messenger was breathing heavily.

"Is it an army?" I asked. My heart pounded against my chest.

"Nay my lord," the guard replied. "It is only a woman. She is alone and seems to be in distress."

If noblemen where going to silence me, would they send a damsel? It seemed unlikely. "Bid her welcome," I commanded.

Wensla and I went into our throne room inside the

palace. We stood on the large green carpet bearing the golden symbol of Granes and awaited our guest. When the woman came through the doorway and saw me, she threw herself on the floor at my feet. The guards ran over to pull her away, but I motioned for them to remain in their place. She clutched my ankles and kept her eyes closed.

"Who are you?" I asked.

"I am Lady Ana," she said. "I have come to warn you that if you do not withdraw your support for Leo, harm will befall you and your loved ones."

"Strange that you should be travelling the roads with no escort," I said. "A woman who travels alone and yet remains unharmed by bandits, foreigners, or wild beasts is a remarkable sight indeed." I watched her closely to see how she would respond to such accusations.

She clutched tighter to my ankles. "I had an escort, but they were mauled by mercenaries who support Leo. I barely escaped them with my life. I am in danger even at this hour. I beg of you! Do not send me away!"

I kicked her away from my leg. "Who sent you?"

She crawled toward me and raised her palms in my direction. Her skin was brown like that of a Saracen. She had hair as dark as a raven and emerald green eyes. She was quite beautiful. Wensla pursed her lips and stared at this lovely stranger.

"I came on behalf of my people in Maltivia," Ana said. "My people and I know Archbishop Leo personally. He's been known to take bribes, and he employs private soldiers to injure those who oppose him. If anyone is found speaking against the archbishop, he has their families killed. That is why you hear only good things about him."

"Impossible!" I said. No one was more gentle than Leo. Ana was probably part of a plot to silence me and destroy the good name of the archbishop. Besides, he was known to prophesy future events that always came to pass. What of that?

"What of his visions from Heaven?" Wensla asked. There was anger in her voice.

I looked at Wensla and her eyes met mine. It was as if she read my thoughts. She looked at Ana again with a stern gaze.

Ana shook her head and pursed her lips. "Leo conjures demon spirits through sorcery and magic. They give him wondrous power to foresee the future and do mighty miracles so those under his power will fear him. Leo pays homage to these creatures of hell and promises them his soul if he is made pope." Tears brimmed in her eyes. "My brother was slain by Leo's minions when it was discovered he spied on such rituals." She clasped her hands together and bowed at my feet. "My lord, please do not partake in this folly. Darkness awaits us all if you do not per-suade Regent otherwise. Even now the pope's mind is being manipulated by the dark forces surrounding Leo." She rose up, pointed her finger at me, and her eyes narrowed. "There is a curse from God against you because of your support for Leo."

Wensla and I looked at one another again and said nothing. Could this woman be lying, or could we have been deceived by Leo? It seemed unlikely. Should I trust the cries of a woman I just met, or the friend-ship of an old friend? I could not easily dismiss her warnings. I remembered when I brought evil tidings to Wensla's father. No one believed me at first, and the kingdom of Tiempo was nearly lost because of it.

"I will verify your tales," I said. I motioned for one of my attendants. "In the meantime, you shall be our guest. My servants will see your needs." I turned to the attendant. "Prepare a meal for Lady Ana and take her to the guest quarters afterwards."

Ana nodded and disappeared with the servant.

I motioned for one of the guards. "Set a watch at the door of our guest. Bring me word if she has any visitors or betrays us in anyway."

The soldier bowed and hurried on his way. I took Wensla by the hand. Her skin was milk white and delicate. I felt comfort as I rubbed the top of her soft knuckles with my thumb.

"Do you believe her?" Wensla asked.

I shrugged my shoulders. "I don't know who the traitor is truly."

The sound of an approaching stallion near the manor startled the both of us. Sir Marcus appeared in mere moments and knelt before me.

"What news do you bear?" I asked.

Marcus rose to his feet. "We discovered no plot against your life my lord, but we did find out some-thing that might trouble you."

I held my breath. I prayed the next words from the lips of my seasoned knight would not agree with the testimony of our visitor.

"We came across a fellowship bearing the symbol

of Maltivia. Their bodies had been cut to pieces and scattered throughout the forest."

Sir Marcus tossed a bloody hand onto the floor bearing a signet ring of Maltivia. Some of the blood splashed onto my tunic. Wensla turned her head away from the scene. My mouth flew open. Either the words of Ana were true, or someone was weaving a devious plot against Leo's good name.

As Marcus turned to leave the palace, he looked over his shoulder. "We rescued one survivor of this tragedy. The maiden is faint and cannot speak yet. If she recovers, perhaps she will have an answer for you." Marcus disappeared through the doorway.

"I need to be alone in these matters," I said to Wensla.

"As you wish," Wensla said coldly. She hurriedly walked past me and ran up the stairs.

Perhaps my beloved thought we should face this challenge together. I didn't expect her to understand my wishes. I went into the nearby chapel, walked up to the front, and knelt before the altar. A statue of the crucified Lord sat in front of it. A picture of my chivalrous father hung on the wall behind the crucifix. I had not forgotten the power and comfort of prayers. I signed the cross. I prayed many prayers in Latin that I had learned from Eli. I felt warmth and strength each time I uttered the words. I prayed until the glowing moonlight and the twinkling stars gave way to the yellow beams of the morning sun. A rooster crowed in the distance. I rose from my knees and stood there clasping my hands together. Surely God would not curse me or my family. My heart was pure in His sight.

I heard someone screaming outside. I ran to the doorway and saw a woman carrying a child in her arms. The boy was limp. I heard other cries all around. The priest of the chapel came running up and invited me back inside the building. He was followed by one of the guards. We stepped inside and the priest closed the door behind him. The two men bowed before me.

"Lord Adrian," he said, "there is an evil presence in this place. The people of Granes awakened this morning to find that children, mothers, fathers, and cattle have suddenly fallen sick. It happened during the night. Their bodies are burning as if the flames of hell are overtaking them. They cry for me to pray over them. There is not enough room in the infirmary for all of the people. I cannot help everyone."

"Where is the lady of Maltivia?" I asked the guard. Surely she was somehow behind this misfortune.

The guard smote his chest and saluted. "Our lady guest has been under guard the whole time. She has done nothing. We must be under a divine curse."

"See to it that she remains in her quarters," I ordered the guard.

The soldier smote his breast again and left the chapel.

Beads of sweat formed on my forehead. Everything Ana had told me was coming to pass. My subjects were suffering, and it was all my fault. If my support for Leo was a grievous sin, it was done in pure ignorance. Would God punish me and all of Granes if my intentions were holy?

"Has the injured girl from the Maltivia fellowship awakened yet?" I asked the priest.

"She opened her eyes just this morning my lord," he replied.

I followed the priest to the infirmary. As we passed many dwellings along the pathway, I heard coughing, gasping, weeping, moaning, and screaming from each house. Some were dragging their loved ones toward the infirmary. Others were calling for me to help them. I closed my eyes and prayed this wasn't happening. My chest felt heavy. I had failed my people.

The infirmary was filled with townspeople. Friars stood over them chanting prayers and using herbs to lighten their pain. Those who had no priest or friar with them were calling out to God for mercy and pleading for someone to administer the last rites. They grasped their stomachs and held their heads. Some were pale and some were as red as fire. The stench of fresh blood and decaying flesh filled the room. I winced at the odor. The priest led me to the far end of the infirmary where the Maltivian girl lay. She had fair skin, brown braided hair, and blue eyes. Cuts lined her throat and scratches covered her face. I stood over her and she turned toward me.

"How are you faring my lady?" I asked in a whisper.

She grimaced. "I...feel...pain and..." Tears trickled down her cheeks. They were mixed with blood.

"Who did this to you?" I asked. My heart ached at this pitiful sight before me.

"I...could...not...be...believe it," she whispered.

"I…" The girl gasped for air.

"Who did this!?" I had to know before the secret remained with her forever.

"I saw…him giving…or…ders. It…was…Le… Leo…" The girl's head fell to the side and a death rattle entered her throat. A purple colored liquid dribbled out of her mouth and soaked into the covering beneath her.

The priest ran his finger through it and sniffed. "Strange substance," he said to me. "It is as if she had been poisoned." The priest pulled some holy water out of his tunic and washed his hands. He reached into a pouch the dead girl had around her neck and found a half-eaten greenish black fruit. He opened my hand and placed it into my palm.

"What is it?" I asked.

"It seems that this was merely an unfortunate mishap," the priest answered. He walked away and signed the cross.

This girl saw the archbishop among their attackers? She was possibly poisoned by accidently eating dangerous fruit? I looked at the strange food in my hand and then at the tormented form of this young maiden. My worst fears were coming to life. I tucked the fruit into a pouch I bore around my neck and made my way quickly out of the infirmary. Wensla met me at the doorway.

"I cannot bear this," Wensla said. She had her hand over her mouth. Tears brimmed in her blue eyes.

"We cannot bear this burden alone," I said. "I will summon your father and Eli. Perhaps we can draw wise counsel together."

Wensla walked away with her hand still over her mouth.

I needed sage advice from a holy man and an experienced ruler. If I were under a curse, I wanted to be rid of it. I needed a plan to help the people of Granes. I didn't know what to do next, and I knew my time was running out.

Chapter Five

—◦⋙◦—

"**L**ord Adrian?"

I jerked in surprise at the greeting outside my chambers. Many townspeople had beat against the door of my throne room and begged for help over the last few days. I had no more food to offer and no more medicine. I was weary of the cries. I did not respond.

"Lord Adrian? It is one of your guards speaking."

"Yes?" I replied.

"The Abbot of Dayma and the Lord of Tiempo are here to see you."

"Bring them in through the private entrance, and bring Lady Ana from her quarters. Let no one else enter."

Within minutes, Vigilan and Eli appeared through a side door. I took them into a small side room where I sought counsel. The table in this room was designed much like the Round Table of King Arthur's time. I wished to have the same kind of wisdom and nobility the legendary king had. I needed it now more than ever. Vigilan and Eli took their places on opposite ends. A cup of ale and a plate of bread sat before each of them.

"What witchery has befallen Granes my son?" Vigilan asked. He stroked his brazen beard in his usual manner. "We were escorted into your presence by your soldiers."

"I have cause to doubt our backing of Archbishop Leo," I said. "There is evidence that he commanded the murder of the inhabitants of Maltivia and is practicing dark magic to gain control of all Christendom."

"That cannot be!" Eli blurted out. "Archbishop Leo is a holy man totally dedicated to the glory of God. I spent time with him in Maltivia and saw nothing of the contrary. All of the townspeople loved him so."

"Perhaps," I said. "But is it possible that Leo kept those things from you? Could he have tricked the entire town into thinking as such?"

"Or perhaps our good archbishop has changed," Vigilan added. "You have not seen him in years my dear abbot."

Eli sunk back into his chair and lowered his head. His face flushed. "I cannot believe these things."

Vigilan surveyed the room. "Where is my daughter? Will she be joining us?"

"Nay," I replied. "She is so distressed in these matters; she chose not to be involved in this meeting."

"Whether the accusations against Leo be true or not Adrian," Vigilan said, "there are many kings and lords who are jealous of the honors bestowed upon you for rescuing the entire kingdom. They see you as a lowly dog or a weak child. They believe you have no right to knighthood, let alone presiding over a county."

I understood why some of the other rulers would be envious. Even though Granes was the smallest of the counties in the region, the province of Elos was the largest and most prestigious of any. It is where the king dwelt.

Vigilan sipped the ale that was before him and placed it back onto the table. "They have often aired their grievances to me about giving Wensla to you in marriage." Vigilan's face became red and he pounded his fist against the table. It rattled the cups and plates. "I told those pompous, arrogant men that you were the noblest man I ever knew." Vigilan leaned toward me. "Perhaps they are somehow behind all of this!"

"From whence does your evidence come?" Eli asked.

I pulled the green and black fruit from my tunic and held it out to Eli. "This strange fruit was found on the person of the dying girl who claimed to see Leo. Purple puss came from her lips as she expired. Even though I learned of many sicknesses and cures from my time with you in the monastery, I have never seen this before. Do you know what it is?"

"I have seen this before." Eli took the fruit from my hand and looked it over. "We have such plants growing in the gardens of Dayma. We grow different vegetation to make various cures. I would need to review my herbal books to tell you what this is." He tucked the fruit in his cloak.

"What other evidence to you bear?" Vigilan asked.

"I am a witness of this tragedy," Ana said. She appeared in the doorway and made her way to one of the seats. "I apologize for being late my lord, but I was preparing myself properly to be in the presence of such important guests."

"Lord Vigilan and Abbot Eli, this is Lady Ana of Maltivia. It is her testimony along with that of others that has brought me to such a possible conclusion."

I bade Ana to tell her story to my friends. I watched her come to life. Tears formed again and watered her eyes. Ana used her hands to describe the attackers and what they did to her and her travelling companions. Vigilan stared at the wall with no expression. Eli's eyes widened and he signed the cross as Ana recounted the horrors that befell the people of Maltivia. I did not hear all of her words. I thought about how miserable Wensla was, how I needed discernment in this matter, and how small I was in the midst of this great conflict. Vigilan was right. The rulers and clergy of the kingdom were treating me like a helpless child. So did Sir Marcus. I squeezed my fists at my side and clenched my teeth. I wasn't angry at those who mocked me, but at myself. Perhaps they had just cause to treat me in such a manner. Everything around me seemed to be crumbling, and I was powerless to prevent it from happening.

"Adrian?" Vigilan pointed to Ana. "The lady is asking a question of you."

"My apologies," I said.

"Did you verify my claims my lord?" Ana asked.

I nodded slowly. "My knights discovered what was left of your group, including a symbol of Maltivia. We brought an injured girl into the infirmary who told me that she saw the archbishop himself commanding the attackers."

Vigilan sat back in his chair and said nothing. Eli placed his hand against his chin and bowed his head.

Ana rubbed her forehead. "I am faint from this ordeal. May I take leave of this meeting?"

"You may return to your quarters," I said. "The servants waiting outside will assist you."

Ana nodded and left the room.

"My lord!?" Sir Marcus burst into the chamber.

"What is it?" I asked.

"Some of your knights have been arrested!"

"Arrested? For what purpose?" I leaped from my seat and grabbed Marcus by the shoulders. "Tell me!"

"They disobeyed my commands," Marcus said. "They went about pillaging and looting the kingdoms of those who opposed your words in The City."

"Why would they do such a thing?" I asked.

"My lord, the knights of Granes said they were acting on your orders!"

I released Marcus' shoulders and grabbed my head. "I never gave such commands! Maybe I am cursed of God." I wasn't sure I truly believed that, but why else would all these things be happening to me?

"You are not cursed," Eli said. "This is a trial of the devil."

Eli's soft voice and kind words were like soothing oil, yet I wasn't persuaded that he was right. Could I truly blame the darkness for all these tragedies?

"What is your command my lord?" Marcus asked.

I looked around the room at Vigilan, Eli, and Marcus. All eyes were upon me as they awaited my answer. "Go to Maltivia and see what is taking place there. Remove the emblem of Granes from your person so you will not be taken captive. Once you have completed this task, go to the Dayma monastery and wait for me there."

Sir Marcus beat his chest, bowed, and left the room.

Vigilan approached me and placed his hand upon my shoulder. "You know what you have to do."

I nodded. There was only one thing I could do. Find the answer myself.

"I will go with you," Vigilan said.

I shook my head. "If there is a curse upon me, I do not wish to have you sharing in its misery. Neither do I want you to face the same punishment that I might have to endure. Besides, I need a place to send Wensla as refuge."

"Send my daughter to Dayma," Vigilan said. "She will have better sanctuary there."

I swallowed hard. Vigilan knew nothing about the problems his daughter and I were having. Could I allow Sir Marcus and Wensla to be together at the Dayma monastery without me? That would be the safest place. They would not be allowed to mingle with one another. I reluctantly nodded.

"I will make arrangements for that," Eli said. "I am going with you as well."

"I cannot risk endangering you either," I replied.

"Am I not under the same condemnation as you dear friend?" Eli asked. "I will be where you are, and I will face whatever you face."

I looked at this pale, thin form before me. Eli's friendship was one thing I had always counted on no matter what adversity we faced. Although the journey ahead might be perilous, I welcomed his company. "Very well then," I said. "If I cannot convince you otherwise, then I would be glad to have you as my companion. Lady Ana will accompany us in our travels." I walked over and grabbed a map lying on the table. I pointed to one end of it and then the other. "We must make haste to appear before the pope and resolve this matter."

"You do well not to have faith in this lady of Maltivia until you truly know her intentions," Vigilan said.

"Until I know for sure my lord, I have no other choice. She is the only witness I have to these events." I still wasn't certain I trusted Ana, but everything I had beheld seemed to agree with her tales.

"It will not be easy to gain an audience with God's representative," Eli said. "He is under the care of a physician most of the time."

"Then I will bring a gift of our finest wine," I said. "It will be a peace offering to his holiness, and perhaps it will strengthen him in his horrible sickness."

"Take enough provisions for the entire journey. None of the counties along the way will open their doors to you," Vigilan said. "I have been told that every ruler from here to The City has closed their gates to the Baron of Granes."

"We will be prepared," I replied.

It was our only hope. There was no other place to turn for help. Pope Regent seemed to believe in me, and he spoke for God. Perhaps his prayers and his counsel would bring me through this terrible ordeal.

If anyone could intercede on our behalf and give an answer to these trials we faced, it would be his holiness.

I had one other thing to do while I was in The City. It would be one of the most painful things that I ever did in my life. I would confront Leo.

Chapter Six

Our horses galloped at full stride away from Granes. Wensla and some of her servants parted company with us and rushed toward Dayma. She said nothing about our separation and she offered no resistance. My beloved acted as if she were in a trance. It wasn't like her at all. Townspeople pelted us with rotten fruit and eggs while cursing my name. We would not be able to maintain such a fast pace, but I wanted to shorten the time to our destination and remove myself from this nightmare as quickly as possible. My head was dizzy with confusion, my stomach cramped with uncertainty, and my chest burned with sorrow.

While everyone slept around a campfire by night, I laid there listening to the crickets and wondered about Leo. During the day, we passed villagers from other towns. They either turned in the other direction or cast rocks at us when they saw the crest of Granes. Eli prayed Latin prayers of protection aloud and signed the cross many times. There was an eerie silence when we entered The City. The crowds from the first encounter in this magnificent place were nowhere to be found. A few priests and monks roamed the white streets chanting. I ordered my soldiers to stay with the horses while Eli, Ana, and I made our way to the entrance of the great hall. I raised my hand to knock on the door when it opened suddenly. Archbishop Darian stood before us with several monks dressed in knightly apparel. They had their swords drawn and formed a line we could not cross.

"I am Lord Adrian of Granes and I wish to speak with…"

"I know who you are," Darian interrupted. "And I presume you are here to either see your friend Leo or the pope himself. His holiness is in bed with grievous pains. God revealed to Regent that you would come before us, and he has requested to see you as soon as you arrived. As for the spiritual father of Maltivia, he will join us shortly."

Eli and I followed the archbishop and these warrior monks through the halls of the glorious building. Large statues dedicated to various saints lined the hallway on each side. The pathway leading through this giant hall was decked in red velvet carpet. We came upon a staircase made of marble leading to another hallway at the top. The glass ceiling displayed different colors and beamed rainbow lights into the sanctuary. Doors lined the upper hallway on each side, and we walked to the end of the corridor where a golden door portrayed the Virgin Mother and the Holy Child.

Darian tapped on the door. "Lord Adrian and the Abbot of Dayma have arrived. Shall I send them in?"

"Bring them before me," a weak raspy voice eeked out.

Darian opened the giant door and gestured for us to enter. Pope Regent lay on a golden bed wrapped up under silk sheets. He breathed hard, clutched the covers, and trembled greatly. He was much weaker than the last time I saw him. He held out his hand with the signet ring passed down from Saint Peter himself. I knelt before the pope and kissed the ring. Eli and Ana came forward and did the same. I bowed my head and waited for his holiness to give me permission to speak.

"You came to see me my son?" Regent wheezed. It seemed as if he were in a strain each time he exhaled.

"Yes, your eminence." I held up the wine in the flask. "I brought this as a token of my affection for you. Perhaps it will bring comfort in your affliction."

Darian took it from my grasp and placed it in the gnarled hands of Regent. The pope held it close to his breast and then placed it on the table beside him.

"Thank you my son," he said.

"I have more to say." I bowed my head in submission.

"Speak then," Regent commanded.

"Since our meeting for the election of the new pope, I have been treated as an outcast by the rest of the kingdom. I have been advised that Leo is not the man of God that he appears to be. I thought it to be lies that soldiers from Maltivia slaughtered innocent people. A dying maiden told me that she saw Leo commanding this small army." I pointed to Ana. "This lady of Maltivia was the only survivor of that fellowship."

"It is true your holiness," Ana said. She pulled back the collar of her dress and showed the markings of a sword on her neck. "I saw the archbishop as well. He was trying to destroy us, for we were travelling to Granes to warn Lord Adrian of Leo's cruelty and evil magic." She choked back tears.

"Is this true?" Regent asked me.

"I was slow to believe such tales until strange things began to take place."

"What things?" Darian asked.

"A plague broke out among my people and vexed them sore. Men, women, children, and livestock died at the hands of this sudden infirmity. Many in my county claimed it was a curse from God." I bowed my head. "Afterwards, I heard news that the knights of Granes were pillaging those who had mocked me for supporting Leo." I raised my head and looked into the eyes of the pope. "I never gave those orders your glory."

Pope Regent nodded to Darian and he disappeared from the room with two of the warrior monks. The pope leaned back against the feathers that served as his pillow. "What is it that you desire of me?" he asked.

I fell to my knees and held out my hands. "If I am under a curse, I wish to be absolved of the sins that caused this calamity. And if Archbishop Leo is indeed a son of darkness, I wish to know the truth of the matter." I closed my eyes and awaited his response. I knew him to be a just and compassionate messenger of God. This was the moment I would be freed from this burden.

Silence.

The door creaked and footsteps followed. I opened my eyes and saw the monkish knights holding Archbishop Leo by each arm. He was bound in ropes. It must have been true, and now God had cursed me in my ignorance. Darian entered the room, unraveled a parchment, and handed it over to Regent.

The pope examined it closely and frowned. He lowered it and narrowed his eyes. "What is the emblem of your heritage?"

I remained kneeling before him, unsure of what he was inquiring. Why did his holiness wish to know such a thing? What was on that parchment?

"The crest of Granes," I said softly, "is a lion of gold ready to strike." What did my heritage have to do with my problem? Was it a curse against my family name?

Regent turned the parchment around and held it up for me to see. "This letter was taken from the hand of one of your men by the Earl of Yakanow. He captured your knights as they tried to ambush his forces among the hills." He shook the letter. "It not only gives orders from the Baron of Granes to massacre the supporters of Archbishop Darian, but it bears your signature and your family crest."

I slowly rose to my feet and dropped my hands. An earl had a letter bearing my crest and signature to destroy? Surely the pope would not believe such forgery. Regent stared at me as if he awaited an explanation.

"Your grace," I said, "I see the letter you have,

but I swear by the God of Heaven that I did not give such a command. Someone has betrayed me and used my authority falsely. I admit that there may be a curse upon me for my allegiance to Leo, and indeed my knights may have betrayed me, but I had no prior knowledge of these things."

Pope Regent stared at me and continued to frown. He didn't seem to believe me.

"If I were guilty, would I come to you now for help?" I asked.

"Only if you were seeking to either trick our spiritual father or you came to lessen your punishment through confession," Darian retorted.

Regent sighed. "Given this evidence, I cannot believe you. I also have similar evidence against Archbishop Leo." He turned his face toward Heaven and held up his hand as if taking an oath. "In the Name of our Lord and Savior Jesus Christ, I am compelled to excommunicate you and all those who are with you until I discern God's will in the matter."

I could not believe what I was hearing. I came to find grace and help from the leader of the church; instead I received a curse greater than any I had ever borne. Regent was being tricked. I had to convince him of that.

"You cannot do that!" I shouted.

"How dare you speak in such a way to God's representative on earth!" Darian bellowed.

Hands clasped me by the arms, pulled me off the floor, and held me in a chokehold. The cold blade of a sword pressed into my neck.

"All of you are to leave The City and never

return," Regent commanded. "Leave my presence and may God have mercy on your souls!"

The soldier pulled me toward the doorway. I struggled with him and tried to wiggle free. I lost my footing as I pushed against those muscled arms. The soldier pulled tighter and pressed the sword so close to my throat that it stung. I felt a trickle of blood streak down my neck. I relaxed my body and submitted to his wishes. Eli, Ana, and Leo offered no resistance as they were pulled out of the room by the holy soldiers. Darian stood next to Regent with folded arms and a look of vengeance in his countenance. The pope bowed his head and signed the cross.

"In wrath, remember mercy," I called out. "I will prove my innocence to you."

The soldiers dragged us out of the main hall, down the steps, and past the gates of The City. Our horses and servants were there. The soldier who had me in his grasp threw me to the ground and kicked me. A surge of pain rushed into my ribs.

"If you come back to The City," the knight said, "you do so on pain of death, and then you will suffer in hell as you deserve!"

The monkish knights stood there with one hand at their sides and the other on the hilt of their swords. I picked myself up and slowly made my way to my steed. Eli, Ana, and my servants mounted their horses as well. Leo stood there looking at me.

"Take me with you my son," Leo said in his hushed manner. "If you leave me, I will be slain."

I looked at this gentle man who held his bound hands out to me. If I left him behind, he would be killed. Perhaps it would be suitable punishment for all the chaos he created. Was he really a monster that needed to be murdered? If he was innocent, I would live forever with the guilt of leaving him behind. I desired to bring him with me and watch him closely. I held my hand out for Leo to grab hold. "Join me."

"But lord," Ana protested, "Leo is an evil..."

"Hold your peace," I ordered. "It is my decision and not yours."

I took Leo by the hand and pulled him onto the steed. His hands were still bound, and I dared not cut them loose in the presence of the knights. They might mistake such a deed as an act of aggression against them, and we were in no position to fight. If Leo remained bound, it would be more difficult to escape. He wrapped his arms around my chest and I winced from the pressure of his hold against my battered ribs. I snapped the reins of the horse and kicked its sides. The others in our party followed. The City faded into the distance behind us.

"In spite of what you have heard," Leo whispered into my ear, "I am innocent of all these things. If you do not believe me, then seek God's wisdom. He will give the answers you desire."

I didn't reply. If he were a traitor, I could keep him under my watch and prevent him from carrying out any more evil schemes. If the archbishop were innocent, I could protect him from those who sought to destroy him. No matter Leo's innocence or guilt, we were all excommunicated. To be cut off from the church was to be cut off from God Himself. I could no longer return to my county. The townspeople truly believed I was cursed and sought to murder me. They would never allow me or anyone they thought was associated with me to enter. We would return to Dayma and take refuge there until the official edict came from the pope to remove Eli. Although I did not understand what it all meant, I knew everything and everyone I held dear was in grave danger.

Chapter Seven

We entered Dayma with paled faces. Wensla and her attendants met us on the monastery grounds. Sir Marcus returned from his scout mission to Maltivia. Everyone gathered into the abbot's quarters and sat quietly around the table. Attendants entered and brought refreshments. No one said anything for a long time.

"Do you realize what it means to be excommunicated?" Eli asked me.

"I don't want to hear of this!" I put my palms against my ears. Did Eli wish to pour salt into my festering wounds?

Eli's face flushed and he dropped his head. "I meant no harm Adrian. I just wanted you to know what would befall you."

I lowered my hands. "I am sorry my friend. It's just that my troubles have overwhelmed me." I closed my eyes and pinched the top of my nose between my fingers. "Please continue."

"Of course," Eli said. "The privilege of baptism has been revoked. All support from the treasury of the church has been cut off." Eli paused and waited for a response. "Your county will be cut off from the rest of Christendom. There will be no marriages, no last rites, no dedications of the children, and no blessings of any kind for your lands or people."

"It matters not," I said. "The people of Granes have turned against me." My father would have been disappointed knowing that his son was cursed. He was well beloved in Granes and the entire kingdom.

Eli folded his hands. "Your marriage to Wensla has been dissolved as well."

"It cannot be!" I cried. I could deal with future church privileges being revoked, but would I lose those from the past as well?

"It is true," Eli replied.

"Why is God punishing us like this?" Wensla asked. She went to the doorway and gazed into the distance.

I smelled the sweet scent of roses in her hair as she passed by. "If it were punishment against only me, that could I bear," I said. "I never dreamed this would happen." Even if our relationship was strained, I ached inside at the thought of no longer being married to Wensla. It was as if a part of my heart had been torn out.

"It is not just against you," Leo said. "Your friend Eli has been stripped of his position and all authority in the church." He shook his head. "I myself have lost everything."

"Look at me!" I pushed my seat aside and pulled Archbishop Leo out of his chair. If he brought this misery upon us, I wanted it to end immediately. I held my right hand up as if pledging an oath. "Swear to me that you have done none of these things you have been accused of!"

"My lord,' Sir Marcus said, "the inhabitants of Maltivia have confirmed all that Lady Ana conveyed to you. They are secretly terrified of their presiding intercessor."

"What say you of this?" I asked Leo.

Leo looked toward Marcus and then stared at me. "I have told you the answer once. I will not repeat it again else I betray my conscience."

My face burned hot with anger at his response. There was so much evidence against him. Was he guilty and refusing to admit it? I wished to strike him, but I suddenly felt pricked in my heart. For reasons unknown, I believed this gentle old man. There was evidence against me as well, yet I was innocent.

Ana pointed at Leo. "I beheld all the suffering of those you cursed in Maltivia." Her voice quivered. "I saw you among those that destroyed my travelling companions. Those butchers praised your name as they slaughtered my friends!"

Leo stared intently at Ana and wrinkled his brow in thought. "I don't remember any royalty being in Maltivia. Everyone knows it is a merchant town. I haven't been there for quite some time because I took up residence in The City until my exile."

"Liar!" Ana cried. She ran up to Leo and pounded on his chest with her fist. Leo held up his bound arms to shield himself. I grabbed Ana by the shoulders and pulled her away from the archbishop. She wept as I held her against me. Wensla took Ana over to the table and sat down.

I pulled my dagger out of a pouch and held it up in front of Leo. His eyes widened. With one stroke, I cut the ropes that bound his hands. "We will trust the archbishop until we know the truth for certain," I commanded.

"He is using demon power to manipulate your mind!" Ana cried.

"We will trust Leo until we actually see him commit such mischief!" I repeated. My jaw tightened. It was not her decision, but mine. I was the lord, not Ana. I would not tolerate disrespect from anyone. If I were being manipulated, I would discover it on my own.

"My apologies lord." Ana bowed her head.

"Do I have everyone's loyalty in this matter?" I asked.

All heads nodded.

Eli stood up and placed his hand on my shoulder. "The only way the church will restore you now is to repent of all the things you've been accused of, make restitution for all the things your knights did, and do penance until the pope is satisfied that you have suffered sufficiently for your sins."

I held my hands out. "What am I repenting of? Commands I did not give? Am I to repent of the sins of my knights?" I pointed to my left palm with my right forefinger. "Does not the holy scripture teach that the church should seek truth in such matters as this? And should not the church restore those who have left the fold? Neither ordinance has been kept."

"Jesus Christ is the true head of the church," Leo

said. "It is He who will restore all those who are innocent. His truth will prevail in the end." The old man gazed heavenward and then looked at me. "My son, you will find that those who are mighty or honorable in the eyes of this world and those that seem least or despised in the eyes of men are often viewed in a different way from the balconies of The City in the world to come."

A monk appeared in the doorway with his head lowered. "Forgive me abbot, but there are men at the door of the monastery. They demand to see you."

Eli started toward the threshold but Leo grabbed his arm. "I sense danger for you and the rest of us. You must not go to these visitors."

"Who are they?" I asked.

"Soldiers wearing monk's attire and bearing the crucifix. They are from The City," the monk replied.

"Delay them until we can find a way to escape," I said.

The monk nodded and disappeared from the doorway. I heard loud banging and shouting outside. Everyone in the room peered through the window and saw the monkish soldiers drawing swords and forcing the monks of Dayma backwards.

"What is your business here that you force your way into our sacred grounds?" one of the monks asked.

"Your abbot, Adrian of Granes, and Leo of Maltivia are under arrest for conspiracy and the murder of Pope Regent XII by order of the newly elected Pope Darian," the lead soldier said. "We have already searched Maltivia and Granes for these outlaws, but they were nowhere to be found."

The monks gasped in disbelief.

"How did this happen?" one of them asked.

"Poisoned wine in a gift offered by that sinful Adrian." The soldier bumped the edge of his blade against the monk's chest. "His soul, as of that of all the other criminals, is damned for all eternity both here and in the world to come! If they resist us, we will hasten their journey to the underworld!"

My heart pounded against my chest. How could I have poisoned Regent? The wine was pure. I drank from the same stock before we left for The City. Either someone had poisoned it without my knowledge, or it was an accident that I had no control over. No one would believe me. I heard gasps around the room. "I am innocent," I said. "Someone is conspiring against us."

"Everyone here believes you," Eli said. He pointed to a latch on the floor. "There is a secret way out of these quarters that leads directly into the stables." He walked over and raised the panel from the floor. Dust flew in every direction and the door creaked. "We must escape now." He coughed and waved the dust around. "Do not worry about the gates. The porter knows that if someone forces their way into the monastery, he is to open the gates to assist in our escape."

"You must go to Tiempo and stay with your father," I told Wensla. "It is my life they seek. You will be safe there until I return."

"Perhaps you are guilty," Wensla said. "You have become a stranger to me. I don't even know you anymore." She placed both hands on her head. "I cannot believe this is happening."

Wensla no longer trusted me? I was smitten with rage and hurt in my heart. I didn't have time to argue this point. I motioned for Sir Marcus. "See to it that she is brought safely to Tiempo." I didn't wish for them to be together, but there was no other choice at the moment. Given the accusation Wensla made against me, I wasn't sure if I even cared for her any longer.

Marcus nodded and disappeared with Wensla down the stairs while Eli held the rickety door. Footsteps and shouts grew louder outside the abbot's quarters.

Ana peered through the window and then turned to me. "They are coming this way my lord. I will go with you."

"If you are with us, you condemn yourself," I said.

"It matters not," Ana replied. "Where you go, there will I be."

I motioned for her. "Come then."

I followed Leo and Ana down the wooden steps and across a dimly lit wooden tunnel. Eli secured the latch on the door and followed close behind me. Another staircase stood on the other side leading out of this secret passageway. The floor creaked above us as the soldiers entered Eli's quarters. Large thudding sounds followed. The monkish soldiers were probably searching for clues to our whereabouts, or perhaps they were seeking for this hidden passageway. When I emerged on the other side, I saw Wensla and her attendants mounted on horses in the stalls. We quickly did the same.

"We must ride hard if we are to escape without incident," Marcus said.

I nodded and held up my finger. When I dropped my hand, I clicked my heels against the horse and we shot out of the stables in full stride. Voices shouted at me from behind and called me blasphemous names. The bulgy eyed porter pulled hard against the door. It opened far enough to accommodate our oncoming group. Wensla, Sir Marcus, and her servants took the road that led to Tiempo. I glanced over my shoulder and saw Wensla looking back at me. It was probably the last time I would ever see her. My heart was heavy.

"Where shall we go my lord?" Ana asked.

"We are not safe anywhere in the land, so we shall leave the kingdom altogether." I held my breath. "We shall journey to Bahran."

"The marshlands to the north?" Ana asked.

I nodded.

"We cannot go there," Eli protested. "It is said that demons reside in that dark domain. No man has ever gone to that place and lived to tell about it. The land is cursed."

"If we are cursed, we should be at home," I said. "No one will come there to look for us." I whipped the reins in my hands and took off. "We ride to Bahran."

All of my fellow outcasts chose to come with me. Dread welled up within my stomach. Maybe my enemies in the kingdom were the least of my worries. Perhaps horror and death awaited us at our next destination. We would know soon enough.

Chapter Eight

Our horses slowed to a trot. The lush, rolling green hills were replaced by rocky crags, dead trees, and shallow marshes. The warm bright sun gave way to gray overcast skies and thick fog. The cool, damp air chilled my skin. The smell of algae and stagnant water filled my nostrils. I twitched my nose in disgust of this repugnant odor. Owls perched on dead trees and hooted. Jackals cried out in the distance.

"There must be truth to the tales surrounding Bahran," Eli said. He pinched his nose as if repulsed by the smell.

Three rotting skeletons lay in one of the marsh pools. One of them was face down as if it had been drowned. Another skeleton laid strewn out to the side with its arms stretched out and its skull facing the sky. The bottom half looked like it was ground into powder. It seemed as if someone, or something, had fallen on top of this one and crushed it. The third skeleton was in several pieces as if it had been cut to pieces.

Leo signed the cross. "May God have mercy on their departed spirits."

I stared at the lifeless bones as I passed by them. Would I and my friends be the next victims of whatever fate befell these pitiful souls? I took a deep breath and tried not to think about it.

Pebbles fell from the cliff to my right. A cracking sound and a loud boom like an earth tremor followed.

"Look out!" Ana yelled.

I jerked the reins of my horse as a large boulder crashed in front of me. The horse neighed loudly and stood up on its hind legs. I slid off the horse and fell backward into a giant puddle of mud. The slime oozed up around my cloak and onto my tunic.

"Are you all right?" Leo asked

"I'm fine." I pointed straight ahead. "There is a clearing about two stadia from here. We shall set up camp there."

Eli pulled me out of the mud and we went to the opening just beyond the pathway. The ground was dry and cracked. This area was a large open circle devoid of plants and animals. It made a perfect campsite. We collected a few dead branches lying around and piled them up. I struck two flint rocks together and started a sizzling fire. Chills ran through me because of the cool mud caked on my clothes. I rubbed my hands together and held them in front of the blaze.

"My lord should be careful not to get sick." Ana untied my cloak, walked over to one of the marsh pits, and dipped it down in the dirty water. She rubbed it together, pulled it out, and draped it over a rock near the fire. She sat down across from me and smiled. "Do not worry," Ana said. "Even if there is disease in the marsh, it will disappear when dried by the fire."

I nodded to her kind gesture. Perhaps I had been too harsh with Ana. I knew she did not trust Leo, but perhaps by being in his presence she could be persuaded of his innocence. The sweet, flowery smell of her clothing and her courtly graciousness reminded me of Wensla.

"Truly this place is the haunt of evil," Eli said.

Ana looked all around her. "There is a story of a love sick huntsman who was spurned by a woman of noble birth. She spoke unkindly to this young man. The huntsman was encouraged by friends to forget her." Ana's forehead wrinkled and her face glowed orange in the firelight. "The youth came to Bahran where he saw a woman screaming and running from a black knight. This ghostly knight said he killed himself because the girl had rejected him. After the girl died, she suffered with the knight for showing no remorse at his passing. Every spring the knight would pursue her, catch her, and cut her heart out. The girl would revive again and the chase would start all over." Ana placed her hand on my forearm. "When the huntsman showed this vision to the girl who rejected him, she had a change of heart and married him."

"I have heard dreadful stories concerning this place as well," Eli said. "There is a tale of a knight who stole lands long ago from the Dayma monastery. The abbot never found out, even to the day of the knight's death." He hugged himself near the fire. "Several years later, the knight's sons travelled through Bahran and met their ghostly father. It is said that his armor and spear burned his skin with perpetual fire. When the sons returned the lands to Dayma as he requested, the deceased knight was released from his torments."

"I too have heard haunted myths about this land," Leo said. "A prince who sought adventure travelled with his squire to Bahran on a quest to unlock its mysteries. One evening, the prince awoke to the noise of thundering horses. He peeked through the flap of his tent and saw an army of wraiths marching in battle formation from north to south. The spirits wore gray robes and bore no skin on their bodies. The prince quietly mounted his horse and tried to follow them, but they disappeared. So did the prince. His squire fled in terror and spread the news throughout the kingdom."

"In each case," Eli added, "those who saw these visions died shortly thereafter."

I nodded and said nothing. I wasn't sure if I believed such tales. I knew some of the stories came from greedy church leaders who wished to scare the masses into giving more money or relinquish lands they envied. Unless I saw it for myself, I refused to believe it. I had more to worry about than idle ghost stories. I lost my kingdom, a bounty was probably hanging over my head, and the woman I once cherished believed me to be guilty of crimes I did not commit. She was far away with a knight she greatly admired. Would Wensla fall in love with Marcus? Since we were no longer married, Marcus could declare his love for her. After all, she no longer trusted me. Would the king place someone else in charge of my county? Were the people of Granes still suffering? I didn't want to stay in this abandoned land for very long. Everything that I held dear was in danger of being lost forever.

"Do you hear that my lord?" Ana looked over her shoulder. "There is something evil watching us. If we had some laurel or juniper, we could burn it in the fire and the smoke would ward off these fiends."

I shook myself from my daydream. I cupped my hand to my ear and leaned forward. I heard a low growling noise above us on the sides of the cliff. The sound seemed to be moving around us from above, but the darkness was so deep and the mist so dense that nothing could be seen. Ana hurried to my side, clutched my arm, and ducked. I patted her on the head. Eli signed the cross and cringed. Leo bowed his head and sat silently. The horses pranced around nervously and bobbed their heads.

The growling became louder.

My muscles tensed as I rolled my eyes around at our dark surroundings. I unsheathed my sword and waved it in front of me. The growling surrounded us and seemed to move closer and closer. Leo and Eli stood up and followed the noise with their heads.

The growling stopped and a deafening silence followed.

A cat-like creature sprung out of the fog and barely missed Eli with its lunge. It roared with a blood curdling scream. The horses jumped around wildly and took off into the night. I whistled for the horses but they were already gone. The cat-like demon stood between me and where the horses had been. I held up my hands as if I were holding this beast back. The monster's eyes glowed green and its fangs were tainted yellow. Powerful muscles bobbed up and down in its legs as it paced around us. It was covered with black spots and white fur.

Ana's eyes widened. "It is a spirit beast!"

Eli backed away from the camp and stared at the monster in front of him. The cat creature snapped its head in Eli's direction and moved slowly toward him.

I held up my left hand in protest to Eli's movement. "Don't do anything rash!" I whispered.

Beads of sweat broke out on Eli's forehead. He never took his eyes off the beast. Eli quickened his pace, turned his back to the creature, and ran as hard as he could. The monster screamed and took off in a sprint after Eli. It chased him into a corner. Eli slid sideways into a crevasse inside the jagged cliff. The giant cat slammed into the wall and reached its powerful arm in the crack to swipe Eli. It missed his scrawny form by mere handbreadths. It continued to claw at him and roar.

"No!" I yelled.

The creature turned its attention away from Eli and looked at me. I felt stiff, as if iron shackles were attached to my legs. I gripped the sword tighter and shrugged Ana away from my side. The beast slowly moved away from where Eli was and approached me. I looked around and tried to find something else I could use for protection. I had forgotten to take a shield, and it was apparent now that it might have meant the difference between life and death. The enormous white cat moved closer and closer. Saliva dripped from its mouth as if it were drooling in preparation of the meal it would make of my flesh. I saw the fire to my side. I had an idea. I waited for the spirit beast to move close enough to me.

Closer...closer.

The beast crouched down, roared loudly, and lunged at me. I took hold of a piece of wood sticking out of the fire and pushed it into the face of the cat. I had heard that evil spirits hated fire, so I was sure it would work. The beast yelped and fell back. Some of its hairs were singed and blackened by the flames burning on the end of the log. The smell of burnt hair filled the air. The giant cat continued to scream and paw at me, but it kept its distance.

"Get out of here!" I yelled. I waved the torch at the creature and forced it to retreat even further.

A loud clap sounded in the distance. The beast turned toward the racket and retreated through the thick fog. I wasn't sure what the noise was or why the spirit beast took off after it; I was glad we were out of danger.

I motioned for Eli. "The beast is gone. You can come out now."

Eli emerged from the crevasse. Dirt smudged his face, his robe was torn, and scratches marred his hands.

"Are you all right?" Leo asked Eli.

Eli examined his hands. "I have a few cuts to mend, but otherwise I am fine."

"You saved our lives," Ana said. "You truly are a hero." She walked up to me, held my head with her hand, and kissed me on the cheek.

Her soft lips sent a warm rush through my body. Eli and Leo stared at me and Ana. My face flushed.

"It was nothing,"

"I wonder why the spirit beast left us in pursuit of the noise?" Eli asked.

"I don't know," I replied. "I am more concerned about how we will travel without our horses."

Leo pointed toward the fog. "Perhaps the creature feared that army of wraiths."

I looked in the direction Leo pointed. This was no myth that stood aloof from our camp. A group of shadowy figures faced us with drawn weapons. With no horses, there was no escape.

Chapter Nine

The shadowy figures moved toward us while Eli, Ana, and Leo formed a line beside me. Ana picked up a stone and held it over her head. She cocked her arm backward in preparation to sling the rock like a small catapult. Eli held the torch that I had used to ward off the ghostly cat demon. Leo stretched his hand outward toward these wraiths and silently prayed with his head bowed. I poised the sword in my hand and steadied for a strike. We were ready. If we were going to be killed by dead knights, we were not going to perish without a fight. The biggest figure in the middle moved toward us and away from his dark group. He wore a dingy gray cloak with a hood that concealed his face. This large shadow held a steel pike with both hands. The tip had a sharp pointy hook. The figure stood there and watched us for several minutes without moving. We remained motionless, waiting for these wraiths to make the first move.

"Leave this place!" the chief wraith hissed.

"I'm afraid that's impossible," I replied.

"Leave this place or you will perish!" the chief

wraith hissed again.

The dark army took a step forward in unison.

"Our horses ran away, and we have been exiled from our lands and families," I answered. "Do what you must, but we will fight you to the last breath!"

"Who are you?" the wraith asked.

"Adrian of Granes," I replied. Why would a dead warrior seek to know my name?

Long silence followed. My palms dripped with sweat and I gripped the sword so tightly that my hand cramped. I watched the wraiths the entire time. They never reacted to my nervous stance. The chief wraith shifted the pike to his left hand and used his right one to remove his hood. Underneath was an ash colored helmet that resembled an angry bull. It had a flattened snout and two horns protruding from the top of its head. The wraith removed its bullish head that extended down over the top of its shoulders. A man's face appeared underneath this layer. He had a brown mustache and blue eyes. A necklace bearing a giant sharp tooth hung about the man's neck. He smiled and revealed his rotten yellow teeth. All the other wraiths laid down their weapons and removed their hoods. Faces of men, women, and even children stared back at us.

The chief extended his hand to me. "I am George of Bahran, and these are the misfits."

I looked at his dirty hand and then at his crooked smile. Was this a trap?

"Come now," George said. "I bathed least wonst last month." He laughed with a coarse laughter.

I clasped his hand and shook it. The white cat

demon emerged from behind these robed individuals and approached us.

"Look out!" I said. I pulled from George's grasp and pointed my sword toward the beast.

George turned to the monster, whistled, and motioned with his head. The white cat creature growled and laid down where he had stood. "My apologies for Ghost," George said. "He's my pet leopard. I was fearin ya might harm him, so I fetched him to me. He protects our little group." George walked up to the beast and scratched behind its ear. The cat purred and rubbed against George's hand. "That's a good boy Ghost. I'll feed ya a rat later."

"Who are you and how did you get here?" Ana asked.

"I will answer all yur wanderins soon," George said. "In the meantime, come to our camp and we'll tend to yur needins."

Two of the robed rogues put out our campfire and gathered our things. We followed this rugged band through the thick fog and narrow passageways. Dead limbs stuck out and brushed me as if they were trying to take hold. Frogs croaked from the marshes, crickets chirped among the bushes, and water plopped to the ground from the rocks. Ana reached for my hand and held it. I squeezed her hand tightly. Her skin was smooth and warm. She needed protection, and she was looking to me to provide it. Wasn't that what a lord was supposed to do for those under his care?

We came to a wide black moat filled with sludge. George cupped his hands to his mouth and made a bird like call three times. A bridge lowered from the other side and pounded into the ground in front of us. As we crossed the moat, the rickety bridge bowed under our heavy steps. A camp site surrounded by rocky walls lay on the other side. Tents lined this place and grubby faces emerged from them to greet us. A roaring fire lay in the middle of the camp roasting hanging meat. The robed individuals that brought us back to camp removed their dark attire and revealed their raggedy clothing underneath.

George clapped his hands four times. Several chubby maidens with rosy cheeks came to me and the others with fresh tunics. They brought us to a large barrel secluded inside a cave. Two of them carried a huge pot and poured water into it. Steam rose from out of the barrel. I was the first to bathe and then dress while the others waited outside. My skin felt cool and light after cleaning up. Each in turn did the same. We were escorted afterwards to the middle of the camp where the fire and food awaited us.

"Join us for supper," George said. "Seein that ya have nowhere else to be and nuttin else to do." He laughed and his pot belly jiggled. He wore a faded brown tunic. He smacked Eli on the back and knocked him forward.

I gorged on the meat and picked the bone clean. I wasn't sure what kind of meat it was, but I didn't care. I was starving. It had a tangy taste. I gulped down the wine they served. It was like freshly squeezed vintage grapes.

"Do you treat all visitors this well?" I asked.

"What do ya mean?" George asked. He bit some meat off the drumstick in his hand.

"A hot bath, new clothing, and food fit for a king," I replied. "Yet this place is so…" I stopped myself. I didn't want to be offensive to our gracious hosts.

"Dirty?" George finished. "Foul?" He picked a large crumb off his shirt and flicked it into the fire. "We got spies and pickpockets who travel to the south and take what we want. Those kingdom urchins wuddin help us, so we help ourselves to their goodies."

"You steal from others," Ana said.

George held up his hands and waved them in protest. "Oh no deerie, we only take what we need and what they can afford to lose. We bring none to poverty. God loves cheery givers, so we take from grumpy ones. What do ya think of that my balding friend?" George rubbed his hand across Eli's bald scalp, then laughed again as he smacked Eli on the back. His pot belly shook as he chuckled.

Eli's face flushed and he shook his head.

"Cat got yer tongue?" George asked Eli. He shrugged his shoulders. "Oh well." He stood up and motioned with his hand. "Come here Edward and bring Cecil with ya."

Two young men approached us shoving one another and bickering. They were short with elf-like faces. One had reddish hair and numerous freckles. His ears stuck out like two wings on the side of his head. The other had yellowish hair with a big, flat nose and two chins.

"This is Cecil," George said. He pointed to the red haired boy.

"This is Edward." George pointed to the yellow haired young man.

Edward bowed and flipped Cecil on the ear. "You are supposed to show respect to royalty!"

Cecil rubbed his ear and shoved Edward. "How do you know that?"

"Cause that's what our mother said do when you see a fair knight and his lady." Edward pointed to me and Ana.

Ana's eyes met mine and my face flushed. I looked away as if I were searching for something.

"This is Uther." George pointed to a giant who sat cross legged near the fire. He was bald with a flat nose and a bulky body. "He can't hear nuttin, but he can break a lance in half with his bare hands." George laughed again and slapped Eli on the back.

Eli huffed and scooted along the ground out of George's reach.

George rambled on for a long time and introduced us to all of the strange members of his secluded fellowship. Some had deformities or terrible infirmities. Others were completely destitute of any worldly goods. They all had one thing in common. They were outcasts from society. They seemed to accept one another and seemed happy in this secret place.

A hunchback monk with a pointed nose walked up to us and grinned. His hair looked greasy and was tangled. "Greetings in the Name of the Lord above!" he said. He shook the bottle he held in his hand.

"This is Leofrick," George said. "He's our priest."

"You need to be baptized," Leofrick said.

"We have already been baptized," I said.

"Yeah but was it did right and proper?" Leofrick asked.

"What do you mean?" I asked.

"Like this." Leofrick held his bottle up toward heaven and bowed his head. "Leofrick baptizes thee in the Name of the Father, the Son, and the Holy Ghost." He turned the bottle up and chugged some of the water into his mouth. He swished it around and spit on us.

"This is blasphemy!" Eli said. He stood up and shook the spit from his robe. "This is not proper rites from a servant of the Lord!"

"You're just jealous because you know none about God's mysterious ways like Leofrick does," replied Leofrick.

"Leofrick is so selfless," George said. "He never refers to hisself personally." George laughed again and swung at Eli to pat him on the back, but Eli dodged and walked back to his tent. I had never seen my friend so furious.

Some of the chubby maids gave us rags to remove the spittle from our clothes. Ana wiped it from her hair and Leo dabbed it off of his face.

"Now that you've been baptized proper, you need not worry about your past sins," one of them said.

"You're wrong," I replied. "My past is ever before me."

The maid looked at me strangely and moved on. The mysterious plague in Granes, the loss and betrayal of my beloved Wensla, the death of the pope, and my banishment thereafter haunted me more than my present surroundings. I had to find a way to solve this dilemma in the coming days.

Chapter Ten

———⊗⊗⊗———

"**A**rise sleepy head."

I stretched my body, yawned, and opened my eyes. Ana stood over me smiling. She raised her palms upward as if she were trying to make me levitate.

"What is the big rush?" I asked.

Ana smiled and didn't answer. She pulled me to my feet and out of the tent. I felt comforted by Ana, but I felt guilty as well. I had feelings for this woman even though I didn't want to admit it. Something drew me to her. Although I had made no attempt to court Ana, I felt faint with love when I was around her. Even if I did, Wensla and I were no longer married and my former bride had lost faith in me. Why was I feeling guilty? If Wensla cared for Marcus, then why could I not care for this lady from Maltivia?

"Time for breakfast!" George shouted with his hands cupped around his big mouth. He rubbed his palms together and sat on the ground.

Eli and Leo sat cross legged by the morning fire. Ana and I joined them. The chubby maids brought steaming manchet served on a golden plate. I took a piece and sunk my teeth into it. The soft bread melted in my mouth, and a touch of garlic spice tingled my tongue. I sipped the pure wine from a silver goblet. It slid down my throat and warmed me just as it had the night before.

"Good iddn it?" George used his sleeve to wipe juice that dribbled off his chin. He licked the bread-crumbs out of his mustache.

"We appreciate your kindness and we will repay it in full." I dabbed my chin with my napkin. "Why have you been so gracious to us?"

"We usually scare strangers away or end up killin em," George replied. "When we found out ya were Adrian the outlaw, we knew ya were one of us."

"How did you know that?" Ana asked.

George swatted at a bug flying around his head. "We have spies who travel round the land and bring news of the kingdom. We know bout yur contro-versy with the pope and how there is a bounty on yer heads." George elbowed Leo. "We even know how many times ya scratched yur backside!" George laughed and raised his hand as if we were going to smack Eli on the back. The abbot raised his arm in defense as if warding off an attack. The portly leader smiled and lowered his hand.

"I need a favor from you," I said.

"Say on." George smote his chest and burped loudly.

"Do you have spare weapons and horses?"

George stopped eating and looked at me. "We have erything one could wish for. If we want it or need it, we sneak to the kingdoms and swipe it."

I stood up and propped my right foot up on a nearby rock and leaned my forearms against my leg. "I've got to return to my people and clear my name."

George cupped his hand over his mouth and burped again. "Now that yur one of us, ya ain't leavin."

"Why not?" I asked. I wasn't sure how he planned to keep us here, but I intended to leave no matter the reasoning of this heavy jester.

"If ya go to yur luvins, there is a chance that someone may find out bout us," George replied. "We cuddnt risk that. We have been safely hidin and cared for in Bahran for generations. If we are found, all the nobles and upstarts in the kingdom will conquer us and put us to their meaneries."

"That's why there are ghost stories about Bahran," one of the chubby maids said. She poured more wine from a pitcher into our goblets. "We spread those rumors throughout the land to keep everyone away."

"I vow to all of you that no one will know of your secret kingdom if you supply what we need and permit us to go back to where we belong," I said.

"We promise," Ana said.

Eli and Leo nodded their assent and signed the cross.

George surveyed each one of us like a vulture seeking a dead carcass. "No one who came to us has ever left, and that's how is gonna be!" George no longer smiled.

What could I do now? I knew he was serious. I could try to impose my will on this fat grungy man and his followers, but there were only four in my group. I was the only one who had any fighting skills. There were too many of them to overpower. I had another idea. "I understand," I said. I smiled at him and extended my right hand. "We would be happy to be part of the kingdom of Bahran."

"Good!" George said. He grabbed hold of my hand with both of his hands and shook my arm wildly. "Ya, yur little lady, the old man, and yur bald skinny friend will be happy here." He laughed and looked at Eli.

Eli's face flushed. He slapped George on the back and George's eyes widened. He held his stomach with both hands and laughed. "Yer scrawny friend has a backbone!"

For the next several weeks, the four of us helped the misfits with various chores. The cool foggy dampness of this place gave way to warmer days where the air was thick. I would often sneak away and scout my surroundings. It reminded me of my days in the monastery with Eli. I went through the camp and talked to different people as they did their chores. Some of them stitched their own clothing, some of them dug into the earth seeking valuable treasures, and some hunted for food. I greeted them, briefly talked to these workers, and moved onward. I wanted them to think I was getting to know my new surroundings better. No one suspected I was forming a plan of escape. This delay would only serve to our advantage. Our enemies would eventually abandon the search for us, and any of the misfits' doubts about us would be put to rest.

One afternoon, I peeped inside one of the tents

and found Uther the giant wielding a large hammer. He pulled a red hot steel rod from the fire and forged it into a sword. Beads of sweat drenched his body, and his shirt was damp with perspiration. He looked at me for a brief moment while he wiped the water from his brow. He looked down again and continued to hammer on the sword. Several weapons hung on iron hooks along the wall. When I walked out of the tent, I heard a horse neighing. I saw holes dug into nearby cliffs that formed stalls. Edward and Cecil groomed the horses and fed them. The breed seemed to be of magnificent stock and well kept. The twins also combed the fur of Ghost as the beast lay there purring in one of the stalls. The brothers bickered with one another as they worked. I found what I was looking for. I returned to my tent to await nightfall.

I watched from my tent until I saw all the lights in the camp go out. I strapped my sword to my side and tiptoed to the tents of Ana, Eli, and Leo. I awakened them and silently motioned for them to follow me. They did so without making a sound. The sky was clear with a full moon and bright twinkling stars. We had enough light to see our way through the camp. We walked in silence until we were far enough away from all the tents.

"What did you bring us out here for?" Eli quietly asked.

I looked both ways. "Since these misfits won't let us go freely, we will sneak out. I know where their armory and their stables are. We can take what we need and be off before anyone is aware of it."

Eli shook his head. "I don't think we will be able

to escape. You heard what George said. Besides, you are the only one who knows how to wield a weapon."

"I have surveyed the whereabouts of everyone. If we don't leave now, we will forever lose everything we hold dear," I said. "It is time for us to reclaim what is ours."

"We're with you," Ana whispered. "I have wielded a sword before."

Eli shrugged his shoulders and shook his head. Leo nodded.

"It is settled then," I said. "Follow me."

We walked past more tents and snoring people. I heard commotion from behind the trees and I held out my hand for the others to stop. We stood frozen til the noise passed. I looked all around me. I felt like we were being watched, but I never saw anyone. Ana and I sneaked into the armory tent where Uther lay on a straw bed with his arms folded. I took a lance and a spear from the nearby table. Ana took a sword from the same table. The lance slid from my hand and clanged against the ground. We froze and looked toward the giant. He never moved. I slowly picked up the lance and we made our way outside. I handed the lance to Eli and the spear to Leo.

I ventured toward the stables with my companions following close behind. The horses bobbed their heads, so I placed my finger against my lips to try to quiet them. There was no sign of Ghost. I prayed he would not be there. Ana, Eli, and Leo stood by and watched. The mares stood still but their ears perked up. They looked sideways out of the corner of their eyes. I wasn't sure what made them quiet, but it didn't matter. In a few minutes, we would be out of this dreary place and headed back to our troubled kingdoms. I reached out and took hold of the saddle sitting across the fence behind the horses. It was in a dark corner. I yanked on the strap, but it was stuck. I pulled harder, and the force of doing so knocked me to the ground. Three figures stood over me extending their hands. It wasn't Ana, Leo, and Eli.

"Taking a night ride are you?" one of the figures asked.

It was Edward, Cecil, and Leofrick. They pulled me off the ground as I clutched the saddle. Ana, Eli, and Leo joined us.

"Now you wouldn't be trying to run away would you?" Cecil asked.

"Even if we are, the three of you cannot stop us," I replied.

"You're right bout that," Cecil said, "so I'll make a bargain with you."

"What do you think you're doing?" Edward asked. He flipped Cecil's ear. "You don't make deals with strangers! They'll tell everyone bout us!"

Cecil smacked Edward's face. "Be quiet you buffoon!"

Edward rubbed his jaw and grumbled.

"What is your proposal?" I asked.

"Me, my brother, and Leofrick were bout to go into the kingdom and do some plundering. If you go and help us, we won't tell anyone bout this."

"What if I refuse?" I asked. "By the time you warn anyone else, we would be long gone." I had outsmarted them.

"Right again," Edward said, "but whose to stop us from telling those in the kingdom where you are? We have spies all over the place. How do you think we knew who you were?"

I was beaten. If I didn't go with them, they might tell George and the others, and then we would be watched constantly. Escape would be impossible. If we did over power them, we might make it into the kingdom and be discovered because of these informants. Even if I did tell the world about the misfits of Bahran, no one would believe a heretic. I could not bribe them. Did these misfits have that many spies in the land? Could I trust them? I wasn't sure of the answer to either question. I had to go along. I extended my hand. "I swear an oath with you."

"That be not the way to seal a pact," Leofrick said. He pulled a rotten fish out of his cloak. "We must all kiss this."

"This is sacrilegious!" Eli said. "Adrian, I don't think…"

"Just do what is necessary," I pleaded with my friend.

Eli closed his eyes and kissed the fish. Leo and Ana kissed it, as did Edward and Cecil. I puckered my lips and kissed it. The fish was soured and slimy. I spit the residue from my mouth.

"Now we are bound before God," Leofrick said.

We saddled the horses and rode off into the night. Even if I had to help this band of thieves, I could at least find out what had befallen the kingdom in my absence and plan my next move.

Chapter Eleven

—⦻—

"**Y**ou go that way, and we'll go this way!" Cecil pointed toward trees on the right and rocks on the left. I followed Edward and Ana to the left side of the trail. We all wore heavy armor and resembled a small band of knights. Ana, Leo, and Eli stumbled around awkwardly in their metal suits. I was accustomed to wearing it. Cecil and Edward moved gracefully in their armor. Cecil, Eli, and Leo hid behind the trees on the other side.

"It seems you and your brother has worn the metal before," I told Edward. "Why adorn the armor? There are no knights among your kind." I was amazed that these ruffians prospered so well. They had no skill and no learning.

"Think about it." Edward removed his mask and pointed to it. "Anyone we attack will think we are real knights and will retreat from our advance. It also serves as protection from weapons our givers might have, and…"

"And," Ana interrupted, "no one will recognize you in these suits."

"Right bout that lass!" Edward winked at Ana and

put his mask back on.

I nodded. It was a good strategy, but I still wasn't convinced that this was a good idea. If these feisty midgets were ever discovered, they could easily be cut down by a skilled swordsman. I considered betraying them, but I wasn't sure what might follow. I didn't want to endanger my friends.

"Now what?" I asked.

Edward examined a small hourglass in his hand. "Now we wait for travelers bearing provisions and trinkets."

"Where is Leofrick?" Ana asked.

"He will be with us shortly," Edward replied.

We waited for a long time. My muscles ached from sitting still in the armored suit for so long. The metal dug into my shoulders and knees. The dark blue of the night gave way to a light blue sky filled with puffy cream colored clouds. Birds sang from the trees above, insects crept across the wooded floor, and animals scurried among the bushes. The fragrance of pine and flower petals filled the forest as it awakened in the brightness of the new day. After several hours, two carts appeared in the distance. They were drawn by four horses moving in a slow trot. Young men sat on each cart and held to the reins. Their heads bobbed up and down as their eyes drooped in slumber. Crops and digging tools were on their wagons.

"Beautiful!" Edward said.

"It is amazing that there are no armed escorts for these carriers," I said.

"No thieves ever were on this road before so they felt no need for protection," Edward replied.

Leofrick emerged from the bushes and waved his arms at these fellows. He was breathing heavy and grabbing his throat. They shook their heads from their dozing and pulled on their reins. The horses came to a halt.

"Who are you and what do you want of us?" one of the young men asked.

"Good sirs, Buckminster is suffering from hunger and thirst. Would you be so kind as to satisfy those needs? God would richly bless you."

"Who is Buckminster?" I asked Edward.

Edward giggled. "Buckminster is Leofrick's secret name. It means preacher. He uses it whenever we are on one of our adventures."

One of the young men climbed off the cart and examined Leofrick. He was still breathing heavy and holding his chest. The lad plucked some corn off of the bundle on his wagon and brought it to the heaving priest. When the young man neared Leofrick, he stepped back and covered his nose.

"A thousand pardons kind sirs, but I have been traveling for days and have had no washing."

That wasn't true. Leofrick rolled through horse dung and dabbed himself with it before we left Bahran. He told me it made him seem more like a beggar and he could get more charity from passersby.

"This corn is as the bread of heaven!" Leofrick said as he nibbled on the cob.

"That is Leofrick's way of informing us bout the contents of the carts," Edward whispered. "If it is something worthwhile, we will take it. If not, then we will move on, and the travelers will know nary the difference."

The youth opened his canteen and gave Leofrick a drink. He turned it up and gulped down the offer.

"Truly this wine is like the rivers that flow through Heaven," Leofrick said.

"It is from the vintage stock of the king's own vineyard," the lad said.

"Bless you my child!" Leofrick patted the young man on the shoulder and then fell toward the ground.

The lad motioned for his travelling companion to help him. The other young man alighted from his cart and grabbed Leofrick by the other arm. The two boys pulled the trembling priest off the ground and helped him to his feet. Leofrick bowed down with his hands on his knees, and then he rose up and smiled.

"Get ready!" Edward whispered.

"Allow me to present you both with a spiritual gift." Leofrick took hold of the flask dangling from his necklace. "I have holy water inside that will purify you from all the sins you have committed."

The two young men stood erect. Their eyes widened and smiles broke across their faces. They leaned forward and watched Leofrick intently.

"Remain still and gaze into the refreshing waters," Leofrick commanded.

They nodded and stood as still as statues. Leofrick opened the flask and swiped it through the air. Liquid spewed out and smacked them in the eyes. They screamed in terror and fell to the ground holding their faces. Leofrick looked both ways and nodded to our two parties.

"Let's go!" Edward said.

I followed my companions in their knightly disguises. Our armor creaked with each step we took. Cecil, Leo, and Eli emerged from the other side in the same armor making the same noise. The short, plump thieves climbed on the two carts and motioned for us to join them. Leo, Ana, Eli, and I climbed onto the wagons.

"Help us Buckminster!" one of the young men cried out. "What is that rattling sound?"

"You hear the rattle of your troubled souls," Leofrick answered. "The water has rejected you because of your many sins. If you do more penance, perhaps your sight will be restored." He climbed onto the first cart. "In the meantime, I will see these carts safely to their destination. Where were you headed?"

"To...to the...The City..." one of them moaned. "It is...for...for the yearly pilgrimage."

"It was a tithe to be given to his holiness Pope Darian," the other wailed. "And we stole from the bounty!" He crawled around feeling for the wagon. "Absolve us of this wrong! Please!"

"The sting of the holy water will be punishment enough," Leofrick replied. "Stay here and pray until you can see again."

As we rode away, I turned and looked at the two young men. They were on their knees with their hands folded, rocking back and forth and weeping.

"Excellent catch my Bassetts!" Leofrick said.

"Stop calling us that!" Cecil shouted. His face boiled purple.

"What is Bassetts?" I asked.

"The name means little one," Edward grumbled.

"He always calls us that after each adventure."

"Whenever I used holy water, it never burned anyone," Eli observed. His voice was muffled because of his helmet.

"Besides being a priest, Leofrick is an alchemist," Leofrick answered. "Leofrick used secret mixtures that make holy firewater."

"He means it makes a powerful acid," Edward said.

"How did you know those youths were guilty of stealing?" Eli asked.

"My dear Aldrich," Leofrick said, "spies give Leofrick and his friends this information long before we have such encounters. We only judge the guilty and take from the greedy."

"Aldrich?" Ana asked.

"Wise counselor," Leofrick answered. "And the old man is Aldred, the old and wise counselor."

"Time to go home," Cecil said. He pulled on the reins and turned the horses around.

Edward did the same.

"Wait!" I held up my hand in protest.

"What is it?" Edward asked.

"Did not those young men say these goods were bound for The City?" I saw the perfect chance to find out what was happening.

"That they did, but we are taking this booty back to Bahran," Cecil said.

"The attire of monks is on these carts, and we could sneak into The City and try to clear our names of all crimes," I said.

Edward shook his head. "Why bother? You have

a life with us now. It duddin matter what happens to the kingdom."

I thought of those I left in Granes. I pictured those I left in Tiempo. I envisioned the faces of dying men, women, and children crying out to me. I saw the face of Lord Vigilan and the pain in his eyes. I remembered the harsh words I had with Wensla and how I had longed to make things right between us. The key to solving all these troubles went through The City. I had to think of something that would satisfy these misfits so they would accompany me to that holy habitation. "Think of all the treasures that The City holds," I said. "We can disguise ourselves as pilgrims and bring even more to Bahran."

"It sounds risky," Cecil replied. "We haven't done any scouting for this task."

"Besides, George will whip us for doing it," Edward whined.

"Where's your sense of adventure?" Leofrick asked the twins. He stood up and held his hands out. "If we bring back even more booty, you two will be heroes in Bahran."

"Heroes?" Cecil asked.

"Rich heroes," I added. My plan was working.

"Then to The City we shall go!" Cecil shouted.

"We'll be captured, and then everybody will know who we are and then..."

"Stop whining!" Ana said to Edward.

Cecil whipped the reins and turned his cart toward The City. Edward grumbled under his breath but followed behind his twin brother. We were well on our way down the road that led to the heart of this conflict.

Chapter Twelve

Crowds of people packed together as we moved closer to The City. The gathering was larger than the previous one I had encountered. I pulled my hood farther down to conceal my face. Everyone in our fellowship disguised themselves in monk's attire. We joined the crowd with chanting while we lowered our heads. Cecil, Edward, and Leofrick shuffled their feet as they looked in all directions. It seemed they had never seen such magnificent buildings before.

"Move along!" a soldier grunted. He waved us through the massive gates of this enormous city.

Edward reached out to take some jewels dangling from the belt of a bishop. The clergyman's back was turned talking to another bishop. The man wore a cape lined with silver and the jewels glistened in the sunlight. Edward pulled his hand in quickly when his would be victim took notice.

I quickly put my arm between the bishop and Edward. "A thousand pardons my lord. My brother thought you had an insect on your person. He wished to swat it from your side to preserve your life."

"Uh…yes, yes," Edward groveled.

The bishop never spoke a word. He turned toward the other bishop and continued his conversation.

"Not yet you oaf!" Cecil elbowed Edward in his ribs.

"In nomen of Abbas, quod of Filius, quod of Flamen." Leofrick chanted strange Latin and signed the cross using head motions. He nodded up and down and side to side. It appeared as if he were having convulsions.

"You are not doing this properly," Eli whispered. "If you continue, we will be found."

I rubbed my thumbs across my fingers in a nervous twitch. These misfits had no courtly or ecclesiastical upbringing. Those around us noticed their unbecoming behavior. Highly ranked cardinals, bishops, and priests raised their eyebrows, rubbed their chins, and wrinkled their foreheads as they watched the misfit monks closely.

Leo placed his hand on Leofrick's shoulder. When the priest looked at the old man, he nodded without saying a word and walked on with his head bowed.

"Eli, ceteri ahead quod nos mos suo vos laxus," Leo said to Eli.

"Etiam meus abbas," Eli replied.

"Come with me," Leo whispered into my ear.

I followed the elder archbishop to an opening between two giant structures. Shadows concealed this alley and the walls were cold. None of the others were with us. What were we doing here?

"Adrian my son, I needed to speak with you alone," he began. "I asked Eli in the Latin tongue to lead the others into the square. I didn't want them to hear what I am about to tell you."

I stood motionless and stared into the face of this old man. His fiery expression sent chills through my body. Leo trembled as he held me by each arm. Was he about to confess his guilt? The commotion from the crowds in the street continued. No one seemed to notice we were there and no one stopped to investigate.

"On the way to this place, I felt the presence of evil spirits." Leo's voice quivered. "Hellish forces seek our destruction. I saw a vision of beautiful creatures with magic powers seducing you and holding you captive to their schemes."

My body stiffened with these words. I had heard of Leo's famed visions, but I never knew I would hear them firsthand and be part of them.

Leo looked toward the sky. "A white light sliced through the gray clouds and pushed them away like strong hands breaking upon a stone. It consumed the creatures and turned their beautiful features into hideous scars and running sores. The monsters fell to the ground and subjected themselves to your rule."

"Why tell these things to me alone?" I asked. I already knew the answer. I wanted to hear it from his lips.

"No one but you must know what I have foreseen. Trust no one my son," Leo warned. "Trust no one but God."

Were these the hallucinations of a madman or a real warning? Who among us was not trustworthy? Was it the lovely Lady Ana? She had given no cause for such mistrust. I had known Eli for years. I refused to believe it was him. Could the betrayal be from my chief knight Marcus? He made a fool of me often but always covered it up with his smooth words and noble mannerisms. Could it be even my former wife? We separated on bad terms. Even though she was angry with me, I could not imagine her having part in such a dastardly scheme. Was it these misfits in hiding? They were a sneaky brood who looked out only for themselves. Was it the people of Granes? They held me responsible for the terror that befell them. Or was it a combination of people? I wasn't certain of anything or anybody.

"I give you my word," I replied.

"Very well then," Leo said. He placed his trembling hands upon my head. "Allow me to pray for you my son."

I nodded and closed my eyes.

"Omnipotens Unus superne, tutela vita illae optimus amicus quod tribuo him sapientia quod discernment in dies advenio. In nomine Patris, et Filii, et Spiritus Sancti. Amen."

I signed the cross even though I didn't understand his words. For the first time in months, I felt warm strength inside and renewed courage to carry on. I had always admired the prayers of Eli, but the conviction in the soft tones of Leo seemed to unlock the gates of Heaven.

"That was a prayer for protection, wisdom, and discernment," the old man said. "God will deliver you from this ordeal and bring you new revelation about life."

What was this revelation? I had to know more.

"What do you fore…"

"Greetings in the Name of our Lord my dear children," a deep voice called out.

Leo pulled me by the arm. We came out of the alley to rejoin the masses gathered in the square. Pope Darian stood on the balcony with his arms open as if he were gathering in all those who were before him. His robes were whiter than snow. A golden cross necklace dangled from his neck, and he held a golden staff with a golden cross on the tip of it.

"I have summoned you before me to give you a message that comes from the very throne of God Himself," Darian began. "Angels carried me into His Presence where I saw the faces of the Christ and His Mother. They placed their hands upon me and commissioned me to be the great intercessor and judge on earth."

The masses applauded and cheered for the new pope. Priests, bishops, archbishops, friars, monks, and other church leaders gazed intently at this powerful man upon the balcony. They seemed mesmerized by his words. They acted as if Darian was Christ Himself.

"The Holy Mother gave me a twofold commission. As intercessor, I will lead all Christendom toward holiness and the celestial kingdom to come. But as judge, I am the punishment of God. If there were not great sins among us, then God would not have sent a punishment like me upon these sinners."

The crowd roared again with approval. I looked around to see if I could find Eli and the others, but they were nowhere in sight.

"By this shall you know that I am God's

representative on earth," Darian thundered. "There shall be great miracles I will perform among you." The pope gazed into his open palms. "Your prayers shall be answered if you do homage to me, but if you spurn the love and care I provide for you in the Name of Christ, then great curses and wrath will be your fate."

The masses raised their fists in the air and chanted Darian's name over and over. A smile broke across the pope's face. He opened his arms wide again and closed his eyes. The chanting continued for several minutes. I surveyed the crowd again to see if I could find my friends. There were too many in this gathering to distinguish one person from another. I was glad no one recognized me. Pope Darian suddenly came off the ground and floated in the air. The crowds gasped. Some pointed at Darian, some fainted, and others whispered their disbeliefs.

My mouth flew open. If this man were wicked, could he do such a wondrous thing? Would not God reveal my innocence to His spokesman on earth? Perhaps Darian's condemnation of me was due to the same evil forces that manipulated Regent. If I pleaded with him once again, maybe his holiness would absolve me of all wrongdoing. Darian slowly descended back down onto the balcony. The gathering grew quiet. Several minutes of silence followed.

"Sancte Michael Archangele, defende nos in proelio; contra nequitiam et insidias diaboli esto praesidium. Imperat illi Deus; supplices deprecamur: tuque, Princeps militiae coelestis, Satanam aliosque spiritus malignos, qui ad perditionem animarum pervagantur

in mundo, divina virtute in infernum detrude. Amen."
Darian's voice rattled in a low hum as he said these
words. It shook the railing around the balcony.

"He's praying for Michael the archangel to take
vengeance on wicked spirits," Leo whispered to me.

"I feel a presence," Darian hissed in a low tone. He
pressed his chin into his chest displaying his silvery
black hair to the on looking church leaders. "The presence of cursed people…the seed of Cain…descendants
of Judas Iscariot…doomed for all eternity…Satan and
his minions have crawled out of the bowels of hell and
inhabited the bodies of these vile beings…"

My body stiffened. Had I been discovered?

"The former lord of Granes, the traitor who murdered members of our Christian kingdom, murdered
our blessed spiritual father, and even abandoned our
lands for the demon lair to the north, is among us…"
Darian opened his eyes and lifted his head to the
crowd. "…as is his wicked allies!"

Heads turned everywhere looking at their
neighbor. I acted surprised and looked around but my
heart beat hard against my chest. The crowd clamored for my death and the execution of all those who
befriended me.

How could Darian know that I was among them
unless it was divine knowledge? Had someone recognized us and informed the pope? Had one of my
travelling companions betrayed me? I wondered once
again if I really were cursed and if Leo was deceived.
I didn't have time to reflect on the matter. Monkish
knights forced their way into the crowd looking for
me and my friends.

Chapter Thirteen

———— ∞∞∞ ————

The monkish knights moved closer to where I was. They removed hoods from anyone whose face was hidden and they examined them closely. The crowds parted to let them pass. I had heard of the devout nature of these men. They were every bit as mighty in battle as they were pious in their faith. They took seven vows instead of three. They held to the normal vows of poverty, chastity, and obedience. They also had the special vows of honor, zeal, piety, and chivalry. If they found me, I would probably be smitten where I stood. I whispered a quick prayer for the help and grace of God.

"Help! Adrian is trying to attack!"

Heads turned toward the noise and the monkish knights froze in their tracks. They moved in the direction of the shrill wailing. It was Leofrick. He thrashed around and held his neck.

"Where is he?" one of the knightly monks demanded.

"He ran away as soon as he heard the pope's decree." Leofrick gasped as if trying to take in more air.

One of the monkish knights offered him water from a cup. He sipped the water and handed the cup back to the giver.

"Where did he go?" one of them asked.

"That way." Leofrick pointed to the opposite direction from where I was.

The holy knights stormed to the place Leofrick pointed at. It was a welcome gesture from the misfit. It gave me time to elude the crowds in secrecy and venture back into hiding until I could think of a way to escape. As I backed away from the crowds, someone grabbed hold of my wrist. A monkish knight whose face was hidden by a hood squeezed my wrist tightly and held a drawn sword in his other hand.

"Come with me!" the holy warrior said.

I pulled myself free from his grasp and disappeared into an alley way. I didn't know where Leo, Eli, Ana, or the misfits were. Maybe they had already been captured. I couldn't leave them to be tortured or killed even if it meant getting caught myself. I was the reason they came to The City and put their lives in jeopardy. I had to think of a way to find my friends and assure their safety. I waited for a moment in the alley but my attacker never appeared. I heard rough voices moving in my direction. I jumped and grabbed hold to a ledge above me on the side of the building. I pulled myself up with all my strength and slid onto this mantle. It was wide enough to conceal my entire body. I held my breath and waited.

"I saw someone come this way!" A screeching voice cried out. Several footsteps pounded through the alley and passed underneath where I was. When the voices faded away, I slowly rose to my feet and peered over the ledge. A monkish knight stood there looking in both directions. I had to find another way out.

The mantle extended around the building. If I followed it, I could be seen more easily out of the shadows. At least between the buildings I was concealed from the sunlight.

"What is troubling everyone so?" someone dressed in royal robes called from a window in the distance.

Monkish knights looked like ants from the streets below. One of them cupped his hands to his mouth. "Adrian of Bahran, the son of Satan, is among us trying to murder his holiness. If you see him, beckon to us and we will apprehend the jackal!"

"The ruffian!" the royal figure said. His voice echoed into the streets. "If I should encounter him, I will smite him personally!"

The figure vanished inside the window and the holy knights marched out of sight.

Sweat covered my body and formed wet spots on my robe. It dripped into puddles onto the ledge. Although the summer heat made the air thick, much of my perspiration came from my tensed muscles. I looked in all directions. My breaths were short and quick. Anyone who spotted me would notice this. I acted as if I were guilty of these charges. I placed my back against the wall of the building and moved slowly along the edge toward a nearby open window. I watched the monkish knight who guarded the alleyway below. He never looked in my direction.

His head continually went back and forth between both ends of the alley.

I bent down on my knees and slithered underneath the window. I slowly rose up and saw a lady of nobility sitting in a chair and combing through her long brown hair. She put down the brush and glanced in my direction. I lowered my head and remained motionless. I heard her footsteps moving toward the opening. If she saw me, she would probably scream in terror and I would be captured. Before the footsteps reached the window, someone called out to her. She acknowledged the call and went the other way.

I crawled across the mantle to the next open bay. I rose up slightly and peered inside. The room contained a table, two chairs, and a bed. No one occupied it. If I stayed out here much longer, I would probably be seen. I slowly climbed into the window and sat on the floor. Out of the corner of my eye, I saw movement on the other side of the room near the curtain. The wind had lifted the drapes up and then back down. I rose to my feet to peer out the other bay. I saw movement again from the corner of the room. The strange knightly monk who had me in his grasp once before pinned me against the wall and held my mouth with his hand. I tried to resist, but he was stronger than I was. His grip felt like iron clamps on my chest.

"Do not resist me," the mystery man said. "I am here to help you."

The stranger lessened his hold and I fell limp. I opened my mouth to speak, but no sound came out. My eyes dimmed from lack of air. This white knight nearly knocked the breath from me. The stranger tossed the robes of the holy order on my shoulder. He peered out the window and then looked at me.

"Put this on quickly and be sure to conceal your face with the hood!"

I was still dazed from his grip, but I removed my soggy robe and put on the holy robes of the monkish knights. It was softer and thinner cloth. I draped the head covering over me and hid my face as the outlander suggested. He turned his back to me as I changed my clothing.

"Are you ready?" he asked.

"Yes," I squeaked. I was still trying to catch my breath.

"Very well then." The stranger handed me a different sword and a large shield bearing the emblem of the cross. "Keep this with you, and do everything I ask of you."

I nodded. My chest was sore.

"Come with me if you want to escape," he whispered. "Do not worry for your friends. They will meet us shortly."

I had no other choice. I followed the mysterious monkish knight through the gathering toward the side streets. I had no idea who I was following or where I was going. If this were a trap, would not the stranger have smitten me already? We walked through small pockets of clergy scattered among the city. We came upon smaller closed gates on the side of the main wall. Guards stood at the entrance. Their white robes and their silver chain mail were familiar. A giant red cross lined their tunics and silver helmets adorned their heads. They had a sword in one hand and a giant shield with a cross emblem on it in the other. More of the holy knighthood.

The knights signed the cross using their swords. "Greetings in the Name of Christ."

We both signed the cross.

"What is your business here?" one of them asked.

Apparently they knew nothing of the tumult happening in the square.

My knightly guide lowered his head and smote his breast three times. "We must make haste to reach the kingdom, for the fallen have fell and great be their fall. The restoration must hasten until the appointed time by our hands."

What was this gibberish the outlander babbled?

The monkish knights held their swords up toward heaven. "The mighty have become weak, and the laborers are few. Godspeed in the quest of his holiness." They unlocked the gate and gestured for us to pass. They touched swords and formed an arch that we passed under. We responded by signing the cross once again. They never asked for our names or examined us.

Four horses stood ready outside the wall with monkish knights occupying two of them. I mounted one horse and my mysterious guide mounted the other.

"Let's go," the stranger said. He clicked his heels in the sides of his horse and took off in a flash.

The other white knights did the same, and I followed right behind them. The City soon faded into the distance. Once we were far enough from our pursuers, I had to know who these rescuers were.

"I suppose you are wondering who I am and if you can trust me," the outlander said. It was as if he had read my mind. He removed his hood. Brown locks fell to his shoulders and a smile broke across his fuzzy face. It was Sir Marcus!

"Greetings my lord," my chief knight said. "I take it you are well. My sincerest apologies for my actions, but I could ill afford to have you discovered."

The other two sacred warriors removed their hoods and revealed the faces of Eli and Leo.

"Where is Lady Ana?" I asked.

"I saw her being taken prisoner by some of the holy knights," Marcus replied. "There was nothing I could do to stop them."

"What about Leofrick and the twins?" I asked Leo and Eli.

Eli shook his head. "We don't know. They ducked into the crowd and ran away."

If Ana were taken captive, then the secret of the misfits might be in danger. The lady of Maltivia could possibly face torture or execution. I had led them into that peril, so I would be responsible if anything happened to them. I couldn't stand the thought of failing Ana after she had put so much faith in me. It felt as if a cast iron plate lay heavy against my chest.

"I know you have many questions my lord," Marcus said. "Lord Vigilan and Lady Wensla await us in Tiempo. We have much to tell you."

It had been weeks since I had seen my former wife and her father. I wasn't so sure if the love between Wensla and I was still intact. Would she spurn me in preference to Sir Marcus? Did she still consider me to be an accursed traitor? Even though I still cared for Wensla, I couldn't get Ana out of my mind.

Leo's admonition still loomed in my thoughts. I was to trust no one but God. It was He who would protect me and bring me into new revelation. This promise was my only hope.

Chapter Fourteen

———⟨⟩———

"**O**pen the gates!"

The guards at the main wall of Tiempo raised the massive iron entrance way. We passed through each gate with our hoods concealing our faces. Though Vigilan remained as an ally, the people of Tiempo probably did not share his sentiments. The farmers and serfs ceased their work and watched us with interest. Mothers and children peeped from their windows as we rode toward the castle manor. The town folk seemed ill at ease with members of the holy knighthood riding through their villages. The guards never questioned us. Marcus had told us along the way that Lord Vigilan had ordered them to make way for our coming.

"We humbly greet all of you in the Name of Christ," the town priest said as he bowed before us. "Our lord awaits your arrival in his council chambers."

Stable boys knelt before us, took the reins of our horses, and led them away to the stables. More guards opened doors for us and lowered their heads in reverence. They treated us as if we were angels from the

Holy City above. It was much different from the scorn, ridicule, and persecution I was growing accustomed to. The guards closed the heavy doors behind us.

A knight approached and saluted us. He had a reddish finely groomed curly beard and reddish brown curled hair. "Greetings my friends," he said. "I am Sir Trentham, chief knight of Lord Vigilan and the county of Tiempo. We've been expecting you."

Sir Marcus, Leo, Eli, and I uncovered our heads. Vigilan entered the hall and extended his hands to me. I took hold.

"It has been a long time Adrian," he said. "When we received the news that you had disappeared into the marshes of the north, we feared the worst. I have lost many good men to that unknown land."

Should I tell Lord Vigilan of Bahran and the misfits? Leo had said to trust no one but God. Besides, I had vowed to George that I would not reveal their secret kingdom, and a man of chivalry always kept his word. I ran my hand through my hair. "It is a dead land filled with corpses, wild beasts, and evil spirits. We lived in fear and prayed often." That was only partially true. Our initial entry to the marshlands was like that, but the misfits treated us to many luxuries. I did not want to dwell upon my adventures. I had many questions to ask. "Marcus, how did you know where to find me?" I asked.

"I sent him out to search for you," Vigilan said. He stroked his beard. "He remained in The City disguised as one of the Papal Knights to learn of your whereabouts and the pope's plans for you."

"Papal Knights?" Eli asked.

"Yes," Vigilan replied. "This order was orga-
nized by Pope Darian shortly after he ascended to
the papacy. There have always been personal knights
appointed to protect the pope, but nothing like this.
Darian claimed that God visited him in a dream and
commanded him to form an army that would destroy
all the enemies of Christendom. It grew from merely
a handful of men to being the largest force in all the
land. They live by the words of Jesus. The kingdom of
God suffers violence, and the violent take it by force."

"When I learned of the order, I joined to clear
my ties with you so I could move freely throughout
the kingdom and be absolved of the supposed curse,"
Marcus said. "All the strange words you heard me
speak to my divine brethren are known only to those
within the ranks of the Papal Knights."

"Marcus and I thought it best that he remain
among them so we could find you first and rescue
you from their clutches," Vigilan said.

"For the first few months, the Papal Knights ran-
domly searched throughout the kingdom for the three
of you," Sir Trentham said. "When they learned you
disappeared into the marshlands of the north, they
abandoned the crusade and assumed all of you were
killed."

"If everyone presumed we were dead, then how
did Darian know we were in The City?" I asked. I
looked for any signs of hesitation from everyone
present. There was none.

"Perhaps there is a spy," Sir Trentham said. "After
all, there is a large bounty on your heads."

"Or perhaps it was supernatural insight," Eli

added.

"When Darian first rose to power, he swore eternal vengeance against you and all those associated with you," Vigilan said. "I tried to…"

"Where is Wensla?" I interrupted. I would never forgive myself if something had happened to her.

Vigilan shook his head. "Alas my poor daughter! I sent her to the women's quarters of the Dayma monastery. She resisted the idea, and many hours of argument followed."

I smiled. Wensla always had a fighting spirit. That wasn't the first time she had been stubborn with her father. I had encountered her bold and outspoken manner during our marriage. At times it had been frustrating, but it also made me proud to witness such strength in a lady of the court.

"That was the only way I could protect her from the wrath of the papacy," Vigilan continued. "She had to do penance for a while to absolve the sins of being formerly married to a son of Belial."

I clenched my fists. Although I had been angry with Wensla, she did not deserve to be punished for being tied to me. I wanted to ride off to Dayma and strike down those who would dare to force this on her. Was this blasphemy? The church claimed that his holiness was infallible, yet why would my innocent wife be punished? Why were my friends and I being falsely accused? If it were not for being assured of a quick death or causing suffering on my loved ones, I considered smiting the pope. After all, what did I have to lose? I was already condemned as a heretic and murderer. I would bring living proof to those charges.

"When was the last time you saw her?" I asked.

"Days after we arrived from Dayma, Lord Vigilan asked that I escort Lady Wensla back to the monastery," Marcus answered. "I left her with the abbess, and that was the last time I saw her."

"I sent some of my servants to inquire of her welfare a few days ago," Vigilan said. He placed his hand on my shoulder. "You need not worry. She is well."

"I rode through your county at the command of Lord Vigilan," Sir Trentham said. "I was forbidden from entering into the manor itself, but I heard that the people are in good spirits and fair health. The plague that inflicted them months ago has apparently lifted. I do not know who the king has appointed to preside over them." Sir Trentham's voice was without any emotion.

I missed the people of Granes even if they had turned against me. They had been tricked into believing I was the cause of their misery. If I could see them once again and prove my innocence, I was sure I would win back their hearts.

"Who has charge of the monastery?" Eli asked.

"There have been several abbots in your stead," Marcus said. "One of them stole from the treasuries, one of them got drunk and caused a scene in the nave, and yet another married a wife and brought her into his quarters. Pope Darian appointed the latest abbot himself." He made a circular motion with his hands. "He is a fat man with several chins, crossed eyes, and a gurgled voice. I have never seen him before."

I saw the pain in Eli's eyes. He dearly loved the monastic life. He had known no other home but

Dayma. His dream of becoming abbot had been torn away from him. I pitied my frail friend. He didn't deserve this punishment either.

"Are you well my father?" Vigilan asked Leo. "You have been silent since your arrival."

Leo nodded and waved to the lord of Tiempo. "I am well."

"Gentlemen, you must be weary from your travels. I have rooms prepared for you in the guests' quarters," Vigilan said. "Everything you require has already been prepared for you. I've informed the servants that you are not to be disturbed once you have settled into your lodgings. Keep your faces hidden beneath your hoods until you are out of sight."

"I understand," I said.

I pulled my hood over my head as did my companions. Sir Trentham opened the main door and escorted us to our accommodations. Fruits and bread covered bronze plates that sat on a table in the middle of the room. Four bronze cups filled with wine sat next to these plates. We took turns picking at the food as we drank the sweet wine. As good as this meal was, it paled in comparison to the luxurious feast the misfits prepared for us in Bahran. Four straw beds occupied each corner of our domicile. The windows were high enough that no one could see the courtyard from inside and no one could peer into the room from the outside. Moonlight beamed through the high windows and formed bluish squares on the stone floor. Two lit candles sat on shelves in the sides of each wall. I heard low whispers from the other side of our quarters. Eli knelt next to his bed and mouthed words

I could not distinguish. Once finished, he stood to his feet, signed the cross, and settled into his bed. He lay on his side facing me.

"I'm sorry for the trouble I've caused you," I told Eli.

"You did not cause these things," Eli said. "As I told you before, this is a trial of the devil. Friends must help one another in times of adversity." He smiled with his sheepish grin.

"I still offer my regrets to you," I said to my thinly friend. "Few companions in the world are as loyal as you."

"Although I have not had a chance to consult my books, I think I remember what kind of fruit it was that you gave me weeks ago."

"Say on," I said. I had forgotten about handing the fruit to his care.

"I believe it to be the yield of the Banewort. It is a poisonous plant whose fruit is often mistaken for black cherries," Eli said. "Had I known of this girl's sickness, I could have cured it with honey and water mix."

"So she was poisoned?" I asked Eli.

"Perhaps she had eaten these by mistake," Eli replied. "Or perhaps someone had tricked her into eating it. The venom causes a person to see visions that aren't there, suffer shortness of breath, heave their innards, and makes them susceptible to suggestion."

I didn't respond to Eli. Could it be that the people of Granes were contaminated as well? Was the priest of Granes in conspiracy against me? He would have knowledge of making cures or curses. Did he form this evil plan on his own or was he urged on by someone else? Was it possible to infect the entire town in such a short time? Perhaps it was only the girl who had been poisoned, and perhaps I was just hoping that it was merely a coincidence and that I wasn't really cursed.

"Lord Adrian?" Marcus called to me out of the darkness. "This will be one of the first places the Papal Knights will come searching for you. We must leave tomorrow if we are to avoid any encounters."

"I know," I replied. "We should leave before dawn. Lord Vigilan has provided enough provisions to last for days."

"My lord," Marcus said. "If you, Eli, or Leo are taken captive, the Papal Knights are ordered to bring you before Pope Darian so judgment can be pronounced against you. Thereafter, you are to be beheaded and burned at the stake for conspiracy and heresy."

"That will not happen," I assured Marcus. "Not until I have cleared my family name and restored every one of you back to your rightful positions and possessions."

I looked at Leo. The old man lay there gazing at the ceiling and folding his hands together. I knew he was interceding for me. I could feel his prayers urging me onward. Now that Pope Darian and the whole kingdom were aware of my presence among them, they would stop at nothing to find me. There was one place I could flee where they would not expect me to go. It was a place for which I had burning questions that needed to be answered.

I would return to Granes.

Chapter Fifteen

———⊗⊗⊗———

*K*nock. *Knock. Knock. Knock.*
Loud pounding on the door startled me. I sprang from my bed, hurriedly put on my cloak, and pulled the hood over my head. Marcus, Eli, and Leo jumped out of their beds and did the same. The knocking continued. I opened the door and stared into the face of Lord Vigilan. He was pale and his body trembled.

"I must speak with you immediately!" The troubled lord pushed past me, entered the room, and bolted the door behind him.

"What is the trouble Lord Vigilan?" Marcus asked.

"I received a letter from the pope demanding that I surrender the enemies of the church into his custody or I will be excommunicated and face a siege from the entire kingdom." He stroked his thin beard fiercely. "I sent scouts into the highways to verify this report. There is a vast army just days from Tiempo."

"A betrayer? Or something more?" I asked. All of my companions were with me in the guests' quarters. No one knew we were in the county except for Lord Vigilan and Sir Trentham. Had Vigilan's chief knight informed the pope and his minions? Many knights had recently betrayed their lords and took over their counties. No matter how the pope found out, the fact remained that they knew where we were. They were coming after us.

"I don't know the answer." Vigilan clenched his fist and raised it into the air. "I will not surrender my friends, even if it means losing my entire estate. Some things are worth fighting for." His face changed from a white expression to that of redness.

I shook my head. "I cannot let you do that my lord. It is one thing for me to surrender my kingdom to protect its citizens. It's quite another that you should do the same. You are not the one charged with these heinous crimes. Besides, I have endangered enough of my loved ones already. Perhaps I should surrender myself to their power and then they might let the rest of you go free."

"Impossible," Leo said. "Even if all of us are taken and killed, Darian and his loyalists will still be in power and will try to subdue all of Christendom to his will. It is better that we all remain free in order to restore the church to its former glory."

"It was your choice to go into hiding to protect your people Adrian," Vigilan said. "This is my choice. I will not surrender any of you, and I will not endanger the people of this county either. We will go into hiding together until we discern what to do about this dire situation. I've instructed some of my other knights and bailiffs to keep charge of the county until I return, and I have sent one of my attendants to Dayma to inform Wensla."

"Very well then," I replied. "If I cannot persuade you otherwise, then I welcome you to our inner circle." I extended my hand to Vigilan and he took hold.

Sir Trentham entered the room with two monkish knight robes draped over his arms. "Here are the clothes you requested of the tailor my lord."

"Excellent," Vigilan replied. "Let us adorn our disguises and join our friends."

Sir Trentham bowed to his lord and dressed himself in the robes. Vigilan did the same.

"Follow me," Vigilan ordered.

We resumed our monkish knightly appearance and left Tiempo behind. Sir Trentham rode closely to his lord. Was he a traitor? I hardly knew him, and I still wasn't sure who I could trust in our fellowship.

"What is our destination?" Sir Trentham asked in his monotone voice.

"Inquire of Lord Adrian," Vigilan replied. "He is leading the way."

I pointed toward a nearby mountain. "We will journey to Granes."

"My lord, we cannot possibly go back there," Marcus said. "The whole town has turned against you and the armies of the pope have posted permanent guards at every entrance. Besides, rumor has it that the ruler who replaced you is most popular with the people. Your county is safe and secure during your absence. You and this fellowship would be needlessly endangered. As your chief knight and friend, I only seek your welfare."

"Could we not enter unhindered in our disguises?" Sir Trentham asked.

"Nay Sir Trentham," Marcus replied. "No other Papal Knights are to appear in Granes. We would raise suspicion and the threat of capture."

"I appreciate your concern, but nevertheless we will go to Granes without being seen," I answered.

Silence followed. We rode through a large plain filled with high grass. It tickled as it brushed by my legs. The grass looked like a giant yellowish lake parting as our horses waded through it. I knew we were getting close to home. I had played in this field often as a lad and dreamed of the day I would become a knight. Now I was living out the nightmare of losing my honor, my family, and my county.

"Hold here!" I held up my hand and everyone stopped. A large oak tree and a giant rock stood before us. I dismounted and walked up to the boulder.

"What is it?" Vigilan asked.

"It is here." I tapped the rock. "Come help me move it."

The others dismounted and approached the stone. They pushed the boulder forward. I dug my feet into the earth and shoved as hard as I could. A rusted iron door lay underneath the stone. It had no latch to open it.

"How do we get inside, and where does it lead?" Eli asked.

"It is a secret passage to Granes," I replied. I walked over to the tree and examined the limbs. "The lock is on the inside of the door and it opens…" I bent one of the branches and it made a clicking sound. "… here!"

A loud bang and a grating noise followed. I

moved in the direction of the racket and saw a dark hole in the ground with an iron door waving back and forth. It creaked as it swung. I crouched on my knees and peered into the opening. Moist cool air touched my face. A rope dangled near the top and swayed in this air current. The other end could not be seen as it disappeared into the blackness of the underground aperture.

"I never knew of this!" Marcus said.

"It was only to be used in emergencies," I said. "My father showed it to me as a youth. I don't know what we may encounter in this pit. To the best of my knowledge, it has never been used."

"How shall we see in this darkness?" Vigilan asked.

"With a torch of course," I said. I took two flint rocks out of a hole in the bottom of the tree and put them into a pouch on my robe. I broke off one of the smaller branches and dipped the end of it into a nearby tar pool.

Leo smiled. "Your father thought of everything."

I wrapped my legs around the rope and wiggled my way down. It was coarse and warmed the palms of my hands. I felt the cord shake as the others took hold of it above me. As I reached what seemed to be the bottom, my feet slid on something slimy. I grabbed the rope to keep from falling. The sudden pull jarred my shoulder and sent pain through me like a knife. I dropped the torch and groped around for it. Something tickled my hands as I rubbed the floor. It felt like the ground moved beneath my heels. I pulled the torch out of the slime and struck the flint rocks against the

end of it. Fire sizzled on the end of the stick. I gasped
at the sight. Vines dangled from the ceiling, moss
covered the walls of the tunnel, and light brown mud
caked the floors. Hundreds of beetles, fleas, and other
kinds of bugs crawled all over this shaft.

"By the heavens!" Vigilan exclaimed.

"Lord be with us!" Eli cried.

We slowly made our way through the tunnel. The
vines brushed my head and numerous bugs crawled
all over me. I felt them moving underneath my robes
across my back, my chest, my arms, my neck, and
my legs. I felt occasional stinging from their bites. I
silently prayed that none of them were poisonous or
blood sucking insects. I heard Eli and Leo chanting
Latin prayers behind me. Another rope swung in front
of us at the end of the tunnel. I handed the torch to
Marcus and pulled myself upward toward the top. I
bumped my head against something hard. I held the
cord tight with my right hand and felt above me with
my left hand. It was another iron door. I rubbed my
fingers across it until I came to a latch. I pulled it
open and it creaked badly. The door did not open like
the first one. It slid sideways into an open hole on the
side of the wall. As I yanked it open, beams of light
flooded the tunnel.

"Where does this lead?" Vigilan whispered.

"I do not remember," I said. I poked my head
through the opening and looked around. It was an
empty, thin corridor made of stone. It reeked of must
and had small windows near the tops of the inside
walls. I heard nothing and saw no one.

"Is it safe for passage?" Eli whispered.

"We are safe," I replied.

I pulled myself out of the hole and shook insects off of my robe. Lord Vigilan, the two knights and the two clergy did the same. Despite the summer heat outside, this chamber remained cool. Marcus placed the torch in a nearby nip on the wall. It gave little warmth to this secret icy hallway. I looked to the left and to the right. Passages lay in each corner of the tunnel.

"Perhaps we should separate," Marcus said.

I nodded. "Lord Vigilan, Sir Trentham and Leo will take the corridor to the right. Sir Marcus, Eli, and I shall go to the left."

Everyone agreed and went their respective ways. We went to the end of the passage and turned left. Another empty long passageway with the same window openings lay before us. We traveled down this corridor. The walls were so close together that my robe scraped against the rough walls and stirred up dust from the stone. My nose burned and I sneezed into my robe to muffle the sound. As we neared the end of the passageway, I heard footsteps coming from the hallway before us. I leaned against the wall and peered around the corner.

"Adrian, is that you?" a voice whispered.

I looked around the corner and saw Vigilan, Trentham, and Leo. Vigilan motioned for us to join him. The hallway must have been one large square along the perimeter of the castle. I nodded to Marcus and Eli. We rounded the corner and rejoined the others. Vigilan, Trentham, and Leo stared into a tiny opening in the center of the wall. It was a stone door with a chain locked around an iron handle. I stooped down with the group and looked into this crevice. It was my council chambers we were peering into. Knights wearing the emblem of Granes and strange men in black robes were seated around the table. I didn't recognize them. These soldiers must have been the replacements for my captured men. My priest was the only one I recognized. He too was adorned in black attire. Another figure entered the room and everyone stood up. This person wore a black robe as well and took their place at the head of the table. The stranger cleared their throat and removed their hood.

I could not believe who it was.

Chapter Sixteen

―――――∞∞∞――――――

Lady Ana betrayed me.
Apparently her capture in The City was merely an act. I felt angry and wounded at the same time. I had deceived myself into thinking that I did not care for her. I had fallen in love with the lady of Maltivia and tried to deny it. Eli was right. I allowed my feelings to cloud my judgment. All my troubles started shortly after she arrived in Granes. Had I been wise to this, I would not have allowed her to be so close to me. Her betrayal answered questions I had pondered for many nights.

"The dark ones are the Drakes," Leo whispered. "They are an ancient, secret magical brood who serve the great dragon. They have moved among us for years, trying to gain control of the whole kingdom."

"I thought they were a myth," Eli said.

I could hardly take everything in. Ana was leading an ancient society trying to uproot the kingdom? Perhaps this was what Leo had seen in his vision. Everyone in the council room took their seats. No one noticed our presence behind the wall.

"I have summoned you because the pope needs our assistance," Ana said. "He has promised miracles to the masses, and we shall supply them." One of the nearby Drakes slid several parchments over to Ana. She untied the scrolls and rolled them out. "These scrolls, and many others like them, contain lost secrets that can make the owner very powerful. They contain recipes for curing plagues we have never even heard of, the ingredients for potent poisons and how to make them, maps of hidden treasures throughout the kingdom, and much more."

"Where do these scrolls come from?" a knight with a thick mustache asked.

"It is knowledge gathered from brilliant minds in faraway lands since the beginning of time," Ana replied. "I have used it often to secure or destroy what was necessary for the cause."

The source of this sinister plot was unfolding before my eyes. Lady Ana must have started the plagues in Granes. She must have conspired with my priest to afflict the people of my county. They must have poisoned the food supply because the plague occurred shortly after the evening meal. I had ordered that Ana be fed before retiring to her quarters. It all made sense now. These knights must have joined the Drakes after being promised great power.

"What is to keep us from slaying you and taking the secrets for ourselves?" one of the other knights asked.

"Only a few of us know the location of all the scrolls. You would only have a portion of the secrets. That is not enough to subdue anything or anyone,"

Ana said. "When you joined the Drakes, do you recall what part of the oath was?"

"You are referring to the mark?" The knight bare his forearm and revealed cuts across it made from knife wounds. It resembled the three claws of a dragon.

"Yes," Ana said. "You also ingested something after taking the blood oath."

The knight's face grew pale. "The black seed?"

"It was no seed," Ana said. "It was the egg of an ancient insect which grows and breeds inside its host. It lives peacefully within your bowels until it is awakened by ingesting something we have not revealed. When that happens, it aggressively attacks your body until you rot from the inside out and die a painful death."

The knight jumped to his feet and pounded the table with his fist. "You witch! How dare you do this to me! I will strangle your neck!"

"Any attempt on my life or those in this inner circle will mean instant death for you and your family. You are joined to us for life and you leave only through death."

The knight slowly sat back down and slumped in his chair.

"Relax my friend," Ana said. "We do not seek your destruction. The power and wealth we will obtain from these scrolls is to be shared among all our members. You will have a great portion with us as we conquer the world."

I could hardly believe her cruelty and evil. How could she be part of such a wicked scheme? I recalled all those private conversations we had about life and all those secrets she knew. It made sense. Ana had harmed the people of Granes and had the blame placed on me. She probably cured them and won their favor when she seized power. It was probably she who informed Darian that I and my friends were in The City. What else had she revealed? Had she told of the misfits in Bahran? Why had she pretended to be one of the fugitives? Was she trying to learn other secrets? Ana continued talking about the daily business of Granes and other trivial matters. I envisioned myself standing there doing the same with my bailiffs, my servants, and my knights. I wished for the simple life in Granes. I missed the seasons of games and the laughter I shared with Wensla. I was tired of running and always looking over my shoulder in fear. I longed for my home as it was before.

"Adrian?" Vigilan tapped me on the arm.

I shook myself from my daydream. "Yes?"

"This is your manor," Vigilan said in hushed tones. "What do you wish to do?"

"Any suggestions?" I asked.

"We could rush them and slay them all in a quick flash," Marcus softly pounded his left fist into his right palm. "Then we could disappear into this tunnel without anyone being none the wiser."

"If we did such a thing, we would create martyrs and justify their accusations against us," Eli said.

"I agree. There must be another way." Vigilan stroked his beard. "If we could get our hands on those scrolls, then we would have proof to clear your names."

"Then we will sneak into the manor and take the parchments and any other necessary evidence," I said. My palms were wet with sweat and my chest was tight. I never dreamed I would be sneaking into my own home as an intruder.

Ana talked for a few minutes longer about the jobs she required of each of them, and then she raised her hands over the group. She growled with a man's voice and her pupils rolled up into her head til only the white of her eyes was seen. "Mighty drage, Grant oss kraft til å gjøre alt vi så vil. Gi oss visdom til å styre og styrke til å dominere, slik at vi kan ha herligheten vi alle ønsker. Ettersom vi snakker slik, så ta det videre."

"Does the lady of Maltivia speak the language of the church?" Trentham asked.

"It is not Latin," Leo replied. "She speaks the language of the barbarians in the far northern icy regions. It is a land beyond Bahran." He squinted his eyes. "I believe she is praying for the great dragon to grant help for the Drakes in their attempt for conquest."

"You speak this barbarian tongue?" Marcus asked.

"Archbishop Leo has knowledge of many things," Eli said.

I stared intently at Leo. He seemed to know a lot about the Drakes and their mysterious ways. Was this old man also a traitor trying to gain my trust in order to overthrow me? I wondered once again if my elder friend was more than just an exiled outcast. I was confused more than ever.

The group in the council room rose to their feet, smote their breast, and walked out with their left palm extended face up in Ana's direction. She tied the ribbon around the scrolls, walked out after them, and closed the door.

"Now is our chance!" Sir Trentham said.

I pulled the latch, slid it open, and pushed on the wall. We entered the room and I took the scrolls off the table. They felt like the rough parchment the monks used in the monastery.

The council chamber door swung open. Ana stood before us with eyes widened. Sir Trentham grabbed her by the wrist and held her tight. He clasped his hand over her mouth to muffle her cries. I closed the door.

"We know everything," I said coldly. "We have all the evidence we need to crush your diabolical plot and clear our names. I'm sure the whole kingdom will be surprised when they find out his holiness is in league with the devil."

"It is you who will burn at the stake you witch!" Sir Trentham hissed in Ana's ear.

"If you swear you will not scream or call for help, we will release you and bring you no harm." I held my right hand up. "I swear it by the chivalric code of the knights."

Ana nodded with Trentham's hand still firmly clamped over her mouth. I nodded to him and he lessened his grip on her. She pulled free and straightened her robe.

"Why did you deceive me?" I asked.

"Because you would have tried to stop me," she said. "Neither you nor your friends understand what is at stake. We are not evil. We seek unity and glory in the kingdom as well. Look around you. There is constant bickering in the church and the kingdoms. We offer wealth and knowledge far beyond anything you have ever known." Ana walked up to me and placed her hand on my face. "I care for you Adrian. I wanted you to share in this glory with me."

All eyes in the room turned to me and my face flushed. I felt condemned as if a secret affair had been exposed. I stepped back from her advance and looked toward the wall where my family crest proudly hung. It had always been a symbol of honor and dignity. Even if I were not guilty of the terrible crimes the reigning pope accused me of, I was guilty of betraying my covenant with Wensla. I rubbed the back of my head. "I am loyal to the king and the church. We do not rule by force, but through divine right given by God."

"Blind fools!" Ana scowled. "If any of you join us, I promise you sanctuary and the opportunity to regain what you have lost."

"At what price?" Eli asked. "You've gained power and traded it for slavery."

"Apparently your weak minds could never understand these things," Ana said.

"How could you harm innocent people?" I asked. "You hurt the faith that clergy and common people had in their leaders. You divided families and friends. Do not these things trouble you?"

"It is necessary for the greater cause," Ana said. "For the welfare of the whole, the few have to be sacrificed."

My mouth flew open. Ana sounded like someone I never knew, someone I didn't want to know. "Have you uttered your entire mind to Darian?" I asked.

"I keep some things to myself in case someone takes the notion to betray me," Ana said. "The secret of Bahran is safe with me."

Vigilan and Trentham looked at me with raised eyebrows and wrinkled foreheads. I had kept my word, but I could not control the actions of others. I had to change the subject.

"Why did you pretend to be one of us?" I asked.

"I was chosen by the others to replace you after I learned of your plans and whereabouts," Ana replied. "We could ill afford to have you escape our hands or thwart our agenda. The plan had to reach its full end before we killed you. We had to know where you were and what you were doing at all times. You and your friends have become the scapegoats as we gain control of the entire kingdom. I was hoping you would join us to avert your murder."

"Who are these others you refer to?" I didn't expect her to reveal the names of the other Drakes.

"Their identities are none of your concern," Ana said. "They are in positions of power throughout the kingdom. The secret conquest has already begun."

Could the misfits be members of the Drakes? Were some of the barons and lords in this plot? Was the pope or the king among their ranks?

"It matters not that you know these things now," Ana said. "Soon all of you will be destroyed. One of your own has already revealed his betrayal."

I heard men shouting and marching in our direction. I looked around the room at everyone.

Marcus was missing.

Chapter Seventeen

The footsteps moved closer and closer. Sir Trentham pulled Ana back into his vice grip and clamped her mouth before she could speak. I tore pieces off of my robe and wrapped it around Ana's feet and wrists. She tried to resist as I tied them, but Trentham squeezed tighter and caused her to fall limp.

"They are almost upon us!" Eli said.

Trentham quickly moved his hand as I gagged Ana's mouth. She tried to bite me but I moved my fingers quickly. I lowered my head, picked Ana up, and carried her writhing body on my shoulder.

"We must go now!" Vigilan said.

I followed the fellowship back into the secret corridor. We sealed the wall and moved along the hidden hallway.

"At least they will not be able to follow so easily," Eli said. "The latch opening the door is on this side of the passageway."

"True," I replied, "but I am sure that Marcus made the soldiers aware of the secret entrance. They are probably waiting for us to come out."

"Then we are trapped," Eli said. "We will be forced to remain in here and starve to death, or they will come after us and surround us." He signed the cross. "If this is our fate, may God have mercy upon our souls."

"There is another way." I pointed to the wall on the left side of the corridor. "There is a solitary stone along the bottom of the wall. Someone step on it."

Trentham pushed his foot against the stone. The partition made a popping sound and part of it moved forward. Vigilan pushed on the wall and it swung parallel to the original wall and revealed another tunnel much like the one we were standing in.

Leo smiled and clapped his hands together. "Glory to the Most High!"

"I had forgotten about this tunnel," I said. "It is only now that I remembered it was there." I did not understand why I suddenly recalled this passage my father had shown me long ago. It was probably the prayers of Leo and Eli giving me wisdom.

Trentham pushed the partition until it was back in its original place. It made another popping sound and locked again.

"Where does this lead?" Vigilan asked.

"It will bring us into the stables where we can escape on horseback," I answered.

Ana no longer squirmed. She stared in wide eyed disbelief at the secret chambers. We hurried down the dimly lit corridor. Peeks of sunlight beamed through various tiny cracks near the tops of the walls. Straw and hay lined the floors toward the end of it. It reeked of urine, mold, and dung. Tiny rats and insects scurried in all directions at our approach.

"We must be nearing the stables," Sir Trentham said.

My pace slowed because Ana's weight was bearing into my shoulder. I pointed toward the partition at the end of the tunnel. "There is a crank on the floor. It will open this enclosing much like the gates of many castles."

"Wait!" Vigilan held out his hand in protest. "What if there is someone on the other side of this wall? They would be upon us or would have time to summon for help long before we were able to raise it high enough to pass through."

Vigilan was right. The entire manor was searching for our whereabouts by now. Raising the panel would make a lot of noise, and Ana's muffled pleas for help would be heard by someone. There had to be a better way.

"Turn the crank," Leo said.

We each looked to one another with puzzled glances. Leo stared at me with the same intense gaze I had witnessed when he told me about his visions.

"Are you leading us into a trap old one?" Trentham asked.

"How do you know this?" Vigilan asked.

Leo ignored the questions around him. "Adrian," he said with deep conviction in his soft tones, "do as I ask."

The hair on my arms stood up. What if Leo was a traitor as well? What if he had been lying to me all this time to gain my trust and overthrow me? Did not Ana do the same? He had no knowledge of military strategy. Even if Leo were not a spy, he could be a foolish old man whose poor judgment would be the death of us all. I stared at Leo for several minutes while the others continued to protest. In my heart I knew I should heed to his advice. There was no way of knowing who or what was on the other side of that partition. "Turn the crank," I ordered. Did I realize what I was doing?

"Surely you jest my lord," Trentham said. "You would put our fate into the hands of this old man?"

"Do as he says," Vigilan commanded.

Trentham nodded and exhaled deeply. "As you wish Lord Vigilan." He knelt before the crank and slowly turned it. The wall rose and light flooded the corridor. My breaths were short and my body stiffened. Ana did not move.

"It appears that Lady Ana has fainted," Eli said.

The panel rose higher and higher, but it made no sound. I slowly walked to the entrance and looked inside the stable. No one was there.

"There must be something afoul," Trentham whispered.

Everyone made their way out of the corridor and into the stable. The horses looked in our direction but never made a sound. Saddles were already strapped on five of the twelve horses in the stalls. It was too easy. Were we heading into another trap?

"Are you some kind of wizard?" Trentham asked Leo. "Or shall we soon meet our Maker at your devious scheme?"

Eli smiled and signed the cross. "It is divine leading. God is with us!"

"To the horses!" Vigilan ordered.

"What about the gates?" Trentham asked. "They will either be sealed or closely guarded."

"Ride to the entrance!" Leo said. "All is well."

Trentham and Vigilan looked at me with raised eyebrows.

I shrugged my shoulders. "Let us proceed to the gates."

I made my way to one of the steeds and draped Ana's limp body over the horse. I climbed onto the saddle and snapped the reins. All the others with me mounted their horses quickly and followed after. Townspeople came out of their dwellings and cheered us on. They believed us to be the monkish knights. I saw familiar faces. I was glad to see the people in my county were faring well even if they believed the lies about me. Soon I would restore their faith in me and be among them.

"Open the gates for the holy ones!" someone yelled.

The gate porters pulled the levers and the large bronze doors pushed their way outward. The keepers waved us through the entranceway and out into the meadows leading to the highways. Swarms of Papal Knights were outside the walls of Granes in a defensive stance. They pointed in our direction and prepared to engage us.

"It is the murderous heretics!" the lead knight shouted. He looked around at his men. "How is it that they were able to get out of the manor? Soldiers were supposed to be posted at every possible escape route!"

"Sir, some of the men reported that the heretics

were escaping through another part of the castle. They left their post to assist."

Leo had known all along. Either he was led by evil power, was weaving events to further a twisted plot, or God was truly with him. I didn't have time to ponder which it was.

"What should we do my lord?" Trentham called out. "If we fight them we will be overpowered."

"Adrian," Vigilan said, "what is the layout of the land?"

"The sea is to the east, the plains and the main highways are to the south, the forests are to the west, and the mountains and marshes are in the north," I replied.

"Turn to the west!" Vigilan shouted.

We veered in the direction of the forest. I knew Vigilan's strategy. If we went into the woods we could hide from their search more easily. I looked down at the bobbing body of Ana. Despite all the action going on, she was still in her faint.

"Take them!" a Papal Knight cried out. Several white robed knights came out of the forest like bees emerging from a hive.

"To the north!" I shouted.

We steered the horses away from the oncoming holy army and turned toward the distant mountains. I saw Sir Marcus leading a group of Papal Knights in a full charge from our left side. They were positioned well ahead of us in the direction we were moving. Marcus held his lance high and shouted a battle cry in Latin. His lance gleamed like polished silver in the sunlight and he aimed the weapon straight ahead.

They were cutting off our only escape route. The soldiers from the forest and the soldiers from the manor gates were still in pursuit.

"We are undone!" Eli cried out. "Lord, spare our unworthy lives!"

Sir Marcus and his fellow knights charged past two oak trees. The entire regiment suddenly fell to the earth on top of one another in a large pile. A rope wrapped around both trees had knocked them to the ground, and two midgets were holding it tight on each end. A giant green skinned ogre appeared from underneath a boulder and roared. I jerked my horse in surprise at this horrible sight. All those in my fellowship slowed their pace and gasped. Some of the monkish soldiers in pursuit fell off their horses, some turned and retreated, and others stopped and stared in amazement. The ogre hurled the massive rock at the remaining soldiers who continued their pursuit. It knocked them to the ground and brought their stallions down on top of them. Two cloaked figures emerged on horseback from nearby bushes. One had a red freckled face and the others had blonde greasy hair. It was Cecil and Edward. They motioned for me.

"Time to run," Edward said.

"Let's go home," Cecil said.

"How did you know we were here?" I asked. "Who is that ogre?"

"We've been following you from a distance ever since we left The City," Edward said. "That ogre is Uther in disguise."

"We don't have time to babble!" Cecil said. "We must go!"

The two short strongmen who tripped Marcus and his forces climbed onto the horses behind the twin brothers and held to their waists. Uther the ogre stomped his way toward a nearby hill and came out moments later on top of a small elephant. We rode toward Bahran with the misfits, and I was certain I would face consequences from the misfit leader.

Chapter Eighteen

I told Vigilan and Trentham about the misfits during our journey to Bahran. I told them of their disguises, their customs, and how they maintained their way of life. The lord of Tiempo listened intently and nodded as if he understood why I had previously kept this secret from him. Edward and Cecil cleared their throats frequently as if they were warning me about revealing too much about the hidden kingdom. I looked behind me on several occasions. No one had followed us.

"You have returned!"

We entered the camp during the twilight hours and stood before George. He examined each one of us closely and stopped in front of Vigilan and Sir Trentham. "Ya were not among us before," George held his scabbed hands out toward me. "Have ya told the whole kingdom bout us?"

"Nay good sir." I pointed to Vigilan. "A chief knight of mine betrayed this nobleman and turned all of Christendom against him. He had no choice but to join us in our quest for justice."

Ana struggled with Uther as he pulled her by the arm. Leofrick walked backwards in front of them. He chanted in his strange Latin once again and dangled a raw chicken across her face.

"Tis such shame to treat the lovely lass in this way," George said. "But at least the chicken will absorb her evil. The sins will spoil it ya know."

"Where are they taking her?" I asked. Even if she was a servant of demons, I didn't want her to be abused.

"Yur lady witch friend will go to our prison. It's an alcove sealed off from the rest of the camp," George said. "What did she do?"

"You mean you don't already know?" I asked. Why was this grungy leader asking me? Were not his people spying throughout the land? Why did he not tell me about Ana and the Drakes? What other secrets were they keeping from me? Were they part of the conspiracy against us?

"Nary none," George replied. "We know lots of things, but there is lots we don't know either."

I wasn't sure if he was being truthful with me or not, and I didn't know who I could trust anymore. Until I knew for sure, I had no choice but to take him at his word.

"Duddnt believe me do ya?" George asked. He must have seen the suspicion in my facial expression. He put his hands on his flabby hips. "Oh well, that's yur decidin. I should be flattered that ya think we know it all."

"She betrayed us," I answered. "Do not be concerned though. She has not revealed this place to anyone. None of us have."

"Ya can't be sure of it," George said. "Ya left us after I ordered ya not to go." He stood there tapping his foot as if he demanded an apology.

Who was this potbellied, foul smelling peasant to be telling me what to do? It should be me giving orders to him and the rest of the misfits. I knew if I belittled him or his band, I might be exiled, imprisoned, handed over to my enemies, or killed. I had to be respectful.

"My apologies George," I replied. "I wanted to know the welfare of my loved ones in the kingdom, and I thought if I could clear my name and that of my friends, then we could return to those same loved ones."

"I vouch for his claims," Cecil said. "We spied on them even after we separated. He never told nary a one bout us." He pointed to Vigilan and Trentham. "Not even his friends here." He wrinkled his forehead in thought and rubbed his temple. "At least not until we came to their rescue."

"And who might ya be?" George asked Vigilan.

"I am Vigilan, lord of the county Tiempo and this is my chief knight Sir Trentham," Vigilan replied. "We have been branded as heretics with Adrian and the others."

"Hmmm." George rubbed his chin. "Then ya have a place with us." He grinned with his crooked teeth as he looked up and down at Trentham. "He's a stiff one he is!" George laughed and slapped him on the back.

Trentham huffed and straightened himself. "Commoners!"

I walked away from their ongoing conversation and approached the prison where Ana was. No one guarded her cell. It was made from gnarled tree limbs held together by thick vines. A rusty iron spike sitting inside an iron latch secured it from the outside. I pulled the spike out and the door swung open. I closed the hatch behind me and looked on her defeated form. She sat in the corner of the alcove against a rock with her hands and feet still bound. She spat at me and turned her head away from my direction.

"Do you realize that if the Papal Knights found out you were a witch, they would subject you to an inquisition and burn you at the stake for being a heretic?" I asked.

Ana did not respond.

"You would have been slain by now," I continued. "I didn't want to see that happen to you. I…" I rubbed my arms and bit my lip. The words came out before I had thought them through. I couldn't lie to myself any longer. I had feelings for Ana and I was trying to resist it.

Ana looked at me and a tear trickled down her cheek. "I'm sorry I had to use you," she said, "but my love for you is no lie. I have cared for you from the first moment I saw you."

I turned my back to her and faced a gnarled tree stump. My soul burned inside for Ana. If Wensla and I were no longer married and she had become a nun, was I not free to love another? Why did I continue to feel guilty for having such feelings toward this beautiful maiden? Ana was deceitful and cruel, but I believed she was merely misguided. Perhaps I could sway her to recant of her evil actions.

"You do care for me, don't you?" Ana asked. "If you did not, then why would you be here now? Please look at me."

I looked over my shoulder and saw Ana out of the corner of my eye. She rustled through the dead leaves beneath her and wiggled to her feet. She held her bound hands out for me to take hold. Wet leaves and damp straw stuck to her dark hair and black robes. A light wind blew through the alcove and filled my nostrils with the orchid scent of this lovely woman. I felt myself being drawn to her by an unseen force. She did not treat me as an inferior nobleman. Even though her beliefs were heresy, maybe there was some truth in what she said.

"I only want what is best for you...for us." Tears flowed from Ana's brown eyes and dripped off of her cheeks onto the moist earth.

I turned to her and wiped the tears away from her soft cheeks. She was so weak and pitiful. I wanted to help her. I wanted to love her. My heart burned like fire for Lady Ana. I pulled her into my embrace and kissed her. My lips locked with her soft lips. I felt waves of heated passion rush through my whole body. I felt powerless before her.

"Take these bonds from me," Ana whispered into my ear. "We can make the world a better place. We can be together."

As if guided by a power stronger than myself, I reached down and pulled on the strip of clothing that tied her wrists.

"Adrian?"

Eli stood at the entrance of the prison with his arms folded. I shook my head as if awaking from a dream. I nodded and walked away from Ana. I dragged my feet and walked toward Eli as if I were recovering from a drunken stupor. I opened the wooden door and fastened it behind me.

"I thought her bonds were too tight and I tried to loosen them a little," I lied. I knew what he was thinking, but it wasn't his place to judge me. Maybe we all misunderstood her.

"Come with me please," Eli said. His voice faded as he spoke.

We walked a distance away from the camp and into the nearby fog. It wisped around our legs as we waded through this puffy white river. I stood there and waited for the lecture Eli was going to give me. He would tell me how dangerous Ana was and how I was being disloyal to my marriage. He would leave out the part about how my marriage was dissolved with a woman who no longer trusted me.

Eli pulled a pouch out of his robe. He opened it and poured purplish gray colored grains into his free hand. "I wanted you to see this." He held it up to my nose. "Smell it."

I inhaled the aroma of the purplish gray grains lying in Eli's pale hand. It smelled like the orchid scent that surrounded Lady Ana. Why would Eli talk to me about this? Did he think I was seduced by the lovely fragrance of Ana? I had smelled different perfumes coming from many ladies over the years, but it never made me feel drawn to them.

"Lady Ana is an experienced alchemist," Eli said.

"Her magic is nothing more than her vast knowledge of poisons, herbal cures, and... and... love po... potions." His lip quivered as he said the last two words.

"What of it?" I asked my friend. He spoke of her as if she were some great sorceress who turned me into her mindless slave. If there were any passion between us, it was not the result of a potion.

"If you cook these grains, mix them with other seeds, and make them into a perfume or lotion, they have the ability to attract men," Eli said. "It is called Henbane." He blew them off of his hand and into the night air. "If ingested and left uncooked, it is a deadly poison."

"I am not a fool so easily seduced," I snapped. "If you think that I am being enslaved by the cunning of our lady prisoner, then you are in error."

Eli's face flushed and he rubbed his hand over his bald scalp. "I have always been your friend, and I will always be your friend. I only want what is best for you."

Ana told me the same words only moments ago. I wasn't sure what Eli was trying to prove or what his motives were. No doubt he had been a sincere friend over the years. Perhaps I was being too harsh. Eli just couldn't comprehend love because of his chastity vows. "I am sorry if I was vile with you dear friend." I put my hand on his shoulder. "You have been a true ally for me, but I think you don't understand what is happening."

"Begging your pardon again," Eli replied, "I don't think you understand what is happening." His voice squeaked as he spoke.

I didn't understand? Friend or not, he was insulting my honor. I wasn't one of the lowly serfs, daydreaming minstrels, or deformed jesters to be mocked. These misfits would be expected to be treated in such a manner. My status placed me above that. "You show your ignorance," I said forcefully. "You would never understand matters of nobility."

"Have you forgotten Wensla?" Eli asked. "She still cares for you."

I waved him away. "Speak to me no more of this."

Eli pulled a flask from his hand and placed it in mine. "This was found hidden among Ana's belongings." He walked away and disappeared into the evening mist.

I opened the bottle and smelled the strong scent. It made me feel sick for love. Perhaps I had been tricked by the lady of Maltivia even though I didn't want to admit it. Even if I was nobility, I had acted a fool.

"Adrian?" Eli called from the dense mist.

His soft voice carried through the fog as if a spirit spoke with me. I saw the silhouette of his thin form. I didn't answer him.

"The misfits have done some scouting, and they found out that a woman from the Dayma monastery is on her way to Bahran," he said. "That is what I came to talk to you about in the first place. She will be here three days from now." I heard his footsteps grow softer as he walked off into the night.

Wensla? Coming to Bahran? It had to be her. Why would she endanger herself? She was no longer bound to our marital vows. Even though she had turned against me, I still cared for her. We had become strangers to one another long before we were separated at Dayma. Now that we had been apart for the past few months, she seemed more like a fading memory. How could I face her after all this time? What was happening between me and Ana? In three days I would find out.

Chapter Nineteen

———∞∞∞———

Three days passed quickly. I spent most of it pacing in my tent. I couldn't eat or sleep. My mind churned constantly over the arrival of Wensla. She would be in the camp this morning. What would I say to her after all these months? Did she still love me? What other reason would she be coming for? Vigilan was here. She must have somehow found out that he fled to this place, and she was coming to be with her father. No matter what might happen, I would let her make the first move.

"A stranger is in the camp," someone called out.

I peeped through my tent flap and saw Wensla approaching on a small mule wearing a nun's outfit. She was as lovely and radiant as ever. It reminded me of years past when we were in the Dayma monastery together. We would sneak around and meet even in the face of punishment. We were so in love at the time. Seeing her in those clothes revived old feelings. A misfit with fur covering his face and arms led Wensla's mule forward by a leash. He resembled a two legged wolf. The hairy man brought her to his plump leader. She alighted from the mule and bowed before George. They spoke to one another, but I couldn't hear what they discussed. Vigilan emerged from his tent with arms outstretched and ran towards Wensla. She opened her arms to receive him, and tears flowed from both of them. George shook his head and walked away with the wolf-like misfit. Vigilan and Wensla held each other by the forearms and talked for a long time. I saw their lips move but heard no sounds coming from them. After a while, Vigilan pointed to my tent and Wensla came toward my dwelling. I jumped away from the opening and fell onto my straw bed on the floor. I didn't want her to know I had been watching her or that I had worried over her coming to Bahran. I lay on my side, closed one eye, and barely kept the other open to see when she would appear inside the tent.

"Adrian?" Wensla whispered. I saw her silhouette at the tent opening. The sun shone brightly behind her and caused her to shine like a celestial messenger.

I stretched and pretended to yawn. "Is that you Wensla?"

She came to my bedside and knelt down. "How are you faring?"

I sat up and shrugged my shoulders. "I am doing well in spite of being betrayed and hunted like a criminal." I wanted her to know just how much I suffered from these false allegations. I wanted her to know how bad her mistrust wounded me.

Moments of silence passed. Tears brimmed in Wensla's eyes and she sniffled. She wrapped her arms around me and held me tight. I was surprised by her actions. I slid my arms around her and patted her. I didn't know what to think. Was she grieving over our separation? Was she happy to see me again? No matter what Wensla said or did, I wanted her to apologize first. I was a man of power and honor. I couldn't grovel before her even though I missed her so much.

"Adrian?" Wensla looked at me with tears streaming down her cheeks. "I have been so lonely without you. I'm sorry that I lost faith in you. You have always been faithful to me, to Granes, and to God. I don't know what has happened to us, but I want it to end."

I nodded. I felt my heart melting toward her.

"My father doesn't know this, but I didn't join the nunnery in Dayma for my protection." Wensla wiped the water droplets from her face with her sleeve. "I joined so I could keep watch for you in Dayma. As you know, a lot of news travels through that large monastery. I wanted to be aware of what was happening with you and my friends." She rubbed my arm. "I heard how you were hunted in The City and how you escaped from the hands of the Papal Knights in Granes."

I nodded again without answering.

"It is rumored that you tried to assassinate Pope Darian and the ruler of Granes." She ran her hand through my hair. "I know you would never do such things. There is a plot against your life and that of the others."

"What became of Sir Marcus?" I asked. I didn't want her to know that I found out he was a traitor. I wanted to see how she would react to hearing of him.

"Marcus is the other reason I joined the monastery," Wensla replied. "He desired to have me as his wife since our marriage was dissolved. I admire his wondrous skill and his great boldness, but he is not like the man I married." She placed her hand on my chest. "No man has a golden heart like Adrian of Granes."

I lifted Wensla from the ground and stood together with her. I held her gently by each elbow. "Why did you come here and put yourself in danger? You had no way of knowing what was in Bahran."

"My father sent a messenger from Tiempo to bring me word of his betrayal," Wensla said. "I knew both of you were in danger, and I assumed you both had probably fled to this place. I couldn't stand it any longer." She gripped my elbows tight. "If I suffer or die with you, then so be it. I never want to be apart from you again."

Wensla wasn't the only one who could no longer stand to be apart. A flood of renewed love burst in my heart toward my estranged wife. It wasn't honor that kept me from Wensla; it was foolish pride. Even if my beloved had doubted me before, she had loved me all along. It wasn't about the deeds I had or had not done. It was me she cared for. Water welled up in my eyes. I pulled Wensla close and hugged her for a long time. There were no strange scented flowers drawing me into this feeling. It was real love for a woman who stood by me even in adversity. I held her by the hand and dropped to one knee.

"My fair Wensla," I said. "Whether we have the blessing of the church or not, you are still my wife.

I will be betrothed to no other." I placed my fore-head on her hand. "I once believed that you preferred Marcus to me and I was filled with jealousy. I wish to repent of my rash behavior."

"Forgive me for those times I dishonored you. I have nothing but praise for you my husband," Wensla said. "I could never love anyone but you dear Adrian. I may honor other knights and nobles, but you are the lord who has my heart."

I leaped from my feet and into her arms. We held each other and wept for a long time. I was so happy at that moment. I was ignorant to fall prey to the wiles of Lady Ana. We walked out of my tent hand in hand as if we were married anew. Vigilan, Leo, Eli, George and all the misfits stood there waiting for us. They applauded and cheered as we came to them.

"Atta boy there Adrian!" Edward nudged me with his elbow as I walked by. "You have two women at your beckoning!"

"Two women?" Wensla asked.

"The raven haired beauty in the prison. The other night Adrian and…um…I…" Edward's face flushed.

Cecil smacked him on the back of the head. "Imbecile! Spreading such slanderous gossips!"

I looked down at the ground with a flushed face. My sin had been exposed by a pear shaped thief. What could I say to Wensla? If I lied or hesitated for too long, things would be much worse. I had to confess and repent. "I must tell you about that. I was…"

"Adrian was under the influence of an alchemist deception," Eli interrupted. "Lady Ana of Maltivia is a witch, and she seduced him with her wiles. He wasn't in his right mind. I found Adrian and awakened him from this magical stupor before anything happened between them."

Wensla pursed her lips and nodded. "I understand. At least I am here now to protect my husband from her wiles."

I sighed and nodded to Eli. He was still a true friend. I vowed that I would never again disregard his counsel.

"It is good to see you reunited," Vigilan said to me. "Despite the decree of the pope, we are still family."

Loud cries filled the air. Several misfits had an armored knight tied up with ropes. They dragged him across the ground to where we stood. The knight cursed and yelled at them.

George bent down to observe the thrashing prisoner. "Who might ya be?"

"You pagan pig!" the knight screamed. "Once I free myself, I will slice you into pieces! I am Sir Gibbons of Mormar. I am your worst nightmare!"

George grinned and exposed his stained teeth. "Feisty one iddn he?"

Sir Gibbons pointed at me. "You!" He shook his fist. "You and your friends will burn in the fires of hell after we smite this God forsaken land! We know of your cowering in this dwelling, and we will raze it to the ground! You cannot hide from the wrath of the church and the kingdom!"

"Where did he come from?" George asked the misfits who captured Sir Gibbons.

"We found him sneaking around the nearby moors. He was with several other knights," one of them answered. "We scared all of them away with our haunting ways except for this one." He kicked Gibbons in the shoulder. "He's a stubborn one that refused to flee. We had no choice but to subdue him and bring him here."

"Take him to the prison with the witch lady," George said.

The misfits shouldered the ropes and dragged Sir Gibbons toward the prison. His head bumped against rocks and dead wood lying about. His armor rattled as it scraped the ground beneath him. The knight resumed his cursing and yelling at everyone around him.

George walked up to me and placed his hands on his hips. He was not smiling. "So ya bring strangers to our doors? Maybe that holy maiden with ya brung em here. Because of ya and yur friends, the whole kingdom will soon know bout us. They will try to invade our lands. It would be to our good that we were rid of all ya!"

Wensla was no traitor, but George was right. Even if I had not personally told others about this hidden kingdom, my being here had brought others into their domain. What if there were other spies among us revealing our every move? I looked at the faces of the other misfits. They stared at me with blank expressions and glares of mistrust. If I didn't act quickly, they might cast me and my friends from this place, kill us, or turn us over to those who sought our lives.

"What say ya?" George folded his arms and waited for an answer.

I prayed quietly in my mind for an answer. I

looked toward the prison, at my robes, and at a skull lying nearby. Who among them could I trust? I had to take a risk. "I have a plan that will secure your kingdom and restore ours. I will need help from all of you."

The misfits looked at one another and whispered. It was apparent they were not favorable to my words. They seemed as empty promises. I had to be more convincing.

I waved my hands in a circular motion and widened my eyes. "This plan is filled with trickery. It will strike fear, terror, and confusion into all those who be our enemies. It will mean much booty for ya all."

Eyes widened among the misfits. Mouths opened. Smiles appeared. They stared at me intently awaiting my next words. I had them.

"Here's the plan..."

Chapter Twenty

"We are taking a big risk," Vigilan said.

I looked at a nearby sundial and nodded as the afternoon sun descended over the nearby cliffs. It had been eight days since Sir Trentham departed with a letter addressed to Pope Darian. He had disguised himself as one of the Papal Knights. Eli and Leo had fasted and prayed the entire time. It took only six days to enter The City and return to Bahran, so we expected Trentham to be back much sooner. My palms were sweaty. Was the chief knight of Tiempo a traitor as well? Ana had told me that I was being spied on continually. If Trentham wasn't a traitor and he got caught, the plan would still be ruined and we would be in danger.

"He's back! He's back!" someone yelled.

Sir Trentham rode into our midst, dismounted, and removed the hood from his head. "Greetings to you all." He saluted us in his knightly manner. "I presented one of the Drakes' scrolls to Pope Darian just as you suggested," he told me. "His holiness took the parchment and said it was heresy. He commanded that the scrolls be burned immediately."

"Did you mention Ana?" I asked. If Trentham missed any part, the plan would fail.

"I told him Lady Ana was a member of a brood of sorcerers called Drakes and that they were bent on conquering the kingdom," Trentham replied. "I told him that the Papal Knights in Granes removed Ana and hold her captive, and that I am their representative to alert him of this brewing evil."

"How did he respond?" Wensla asked.

"Darian's countenance did not change," Trentham said. "He handed me a letter of authorization with his seal to cut her down immediately." He placed the papal letter in my hand. "Darian said that Ana cannot go on trial because he did not want her treacherous paganism polluting holy ground. He also told us not to believe any lies she might tell to preserve her life."

"Part of the cover up no doubt," Vigilan said. "Why were you late in arriving?"

"Pope Darian sent other Papal Knights with me for protection and assistance," Trentham said. "These holy knights talked of how Lady Ana and the outcasts of Adrian were spawns of the devil, and how they would put an end to this spreading wickedness."

"How did you escape from your companions?" Vigilan asked.

Trentham pointed to misfits standing near his horse. "I was supposedly captured by these miscreants dressed as Drakes and carried off from the presence of the other knights. We took various routes to confuse them. That is why it was two more days journey before we reached you. I can assure you that we were not followed."

Vigilan, Trentham, Wensla, and I approached the cave-like prison where Lady Ana and Sir Gibbons had been kept. Two misfits stood guard at the entrance.

I knocked on the wooden gate. "Lady Ana? May we speak with you?"

Ana did not answer me.

"We have news," I said. "Pope Darian has declared you a heretic. You are to be cut down immediately for your witchery."

Ana appeared at the doorway of the prison and wrapped her hands around the poles. She stuck her face between them and stared intently at me. I held out the unraveled letter with the official seal and signature of the pope. She glanced at it and then stared at me.

"The pope has betrayed you," I said. "You are a fugitive like the rest of us. The pope ordered that anything you might say in your defense is a lie to be ignored."

"You're lying!" Ana screamed.

I pointed to the seal at the bottom of the letter. "This is the sign of the pope. It cannot be copied. If you leave us, you will be hunted down and killed in cold blood. If you help us, you will at least be given a fair trial and the possibility of your life."

"Adrian," Ana reached between the wooden posts and grabbed my hand. "My offer still stands. If you care anything for me, you won't let anyone hurt me. You know I would do anything for you. Would you do the same for me?"

I froze and gripped the letter tightly. She was

trying to stir trouble. I didn't know what to say.

"His feelings for you were from your wicked magic!" Wensla hissed. "Remove your grip from my husband, or I shall remove your head from your vile body!"

Ana quickly lessened her grip and moved back from the prison door. "I curse all of you with my last breath!" she cried. "I will never help any of you!"

Sir Gibbons laughed. "You fools can play your games for now, but you will be found and butchered. I cannot wait to behold the slaughter."

I looked at Wensla. Her jaw was tight and her fists were clenched. I had never seen her so filled with fire. She defended me even though in my heart I knew that some of my feelings for Ana were not from the effects of her sorcery. I wanted more than ever to be faithful and true to my wife. I guided Wensla away from the prison. Vigilan and Trentham followed us to where Eli and George stood.

"I have been praying for everyone," Eli said. "Has your plan reached fruition yet?"

"We have encountered an obstacle," I said. "The pope played into our trap, but the sorceress of Maltivia is not cooperating. I was hoping that she would become so enraged at the pope's decree against her that she would be a witness against him and reveal their hidden agenda."

"We be in a troubled spot," George scratched his head. "By the way, the old man who came with ya wants to see ya. He's in his tent and he's seein things again."

I left the group standing there mulling in their

thoughts and headed toward Leo's tent. The sun disappeared beyond the horizon and the cool star filled night took over the scenery. I was out of ideas on how to proceed. I needed divine wisdom. If anyone could give me that, it was Leo. I entered his tent and saw him on his knees with his head bowed and his hands folded in prayer.

"You wanted to see me your holiness?"

Leo raised his head, opened his eyes, and turned to look at me. "That designation is meant only for the one who holds the office of the pope."

"In my heart you are that man," I replied. "You bring me word?"

"I know you're plan has been halted," Leo said. "God has shown it to me. He has also revealed a vision. I saw Pope Darian engaged in a loving fashion with Lady Ana. I heard a conversation between them concerning their cover up about Ana being his mistress. I overheard them in his chambers devising the scheme to unleash black magic on the masses while conspiring against me and those who support me. I saw her seducing many men and taking their power from them without their knowledge."

I stared at Leo intently. Pain filled his eyes and passion gripped his voice. How could he know such things? Was this truly a powerful revelation from the Almighty? Deep in my heart I felt it was true. Everything he had prophesied to this point had been accurate. Feelings I had for Ana drained from my body as Divine light opened my mind. I knew what I had to do. It would move the plan forward and prove the truth of Leo's words. "Come with me," I said to my elder friend.

We found George stooping over a fire and roasting a dead bird on a stick. "Mmmmm," he said. He swung the smoking bird toward our faces. "Makes for a hearty meal it does."

"I need a favor from you," I said to George.

"And why would I be a doin that?" George asked. "Ya gonna run off again?"

I shook my head. "It will mean my plan will start working so all of you can have your booty. Will you send your guards away from the cell for a while?"

"Hmmm," replied George. He twirled the ribbon around his neck that held the cat's tooth. "Give the guards my password and they will let ya through." He wiped his nose and sniffled. "Say 'cookaroo' to them."

"What does that mean?" I asked George.

"I dunno." George shrugged his shoulders. "It's just what we say when we want to visit prisoners in hidin."

I shrugged my shoulders and nodded. Leo and I left the portly misfit leader and went to the prison. The full moon gave us ample light to see our way clear. I put my finger to my lips for the misfits who guarded the prisoners.

"Cookaroo!" I said. I felt strange saying it. Was George serious?

They nodded and remained silent. They stood at the side of the prison with Leo where they were out of sight. I knocked on the secured gate.

"Ana? It's Adrian again. I'm alone and I need to see you."

Ana appeared at the entrance of the cell with her arms folded.

I looked both ways and lowered my voice. "I wanted you to know what torture it was seeing you and not being able to return your love." I peered into the prison. "Where is Sir Gibbons?"

"He is sleeping like a tiger," Ana replied in a whisper. "Let me out and we will sneak away and rule the kingdom together."

Her words had no meaning anymore. I had to get her to confess to her devious plot with Pope Darian. I unlatched the prison door softly and opened it up. Ana walked out and put her arms around me.

"I heard rumor that you were the mistress of Pope Darian, and that you plotted all this sorcery with him in order to take the kingdom and ruin Leo and his supporters."

"How did you know that?" Ana asked.

"I cannot reveal all my informants can I?" I winked at her and smiled.

"It is true," Ana replied. "But if Darian has betrayed me, then we shall bring down his rule and reign in his stead." She ran her pointing finger down the bridge of my nose and across my lips. "Do not be jealous though. I prefer you over him. You are much more handsome."

"Yes," I said. "We shall conquer Darian with your evidence and your confession." I removed her arms from my shoulders.

Ana looked to her left and saw Leo and the misfits emerge from nearby bushes. She smacked me across the face and tried to run. The misfit guards caught up to Ana and wrestled her to the ground. She kicked, screeched, and spit at everyone.

"You traitorous swine!" Ana yelled at me.

The misfits dragged her back into the cell and secured the door. An awakened Sir Gibbons grumbled at Ana. She yelled at him. They bickered at one another for several minutes.

"You heard the confession?" I asked Leo.

The old man nodded.

"I heard the confession too." A raven haired woman wearing a black robe appeared from behind a nearby rock. She resembled Lady Ana, yet we heard the witch's voice as she clamored with the grieved knight in the prison.

"Who are you?" I asked. I squinted to see if I could discern this form. Was it some kind of sorcery from the lady of Maltivia?

"It is your lady love." Wensla's face shone in the moonlight. "I dyed my hair with berry mixes and put on these dark robes. If Lady Ana will not cooperate with you, then I will be her replacement."

"Brilliant!" Leo said.

Everything was coming together. Leo had proven to be a messenger of the Lord, Wensla witnessed my faithfulness to our bond, Ana confessed to her wicked plot with Darian, and the misfits had agreed to help.

The final showdown was nearly upon us.

Chapter Twenty One

"We will divide into two groups."
I pointed to a map that George gave me. I ran my finger up the right side and then over to the left. Vigilan held one end of the map and George held the other end. They nodded in agreement. The three of us stood under a large tent with Eli, Wensla, Leo, Trentham, Edward, Cecil, Leofrick, and Uther.

"Wensla will come with me as we make our way to The City," I said. "We will make them think that she is Ana and that she is ready to confess this plot. This will draw our enemies to us and allow Eli, Vigilan, Leo, and Trentham to take the evidence of this conspiracy before the Council of Elders."

"Do you think they will listen?" Vigilan asked.

"The members of the council are fair men who truly love God and the church," Leo said. "Once they have been convinced, the Papal Knights will follow their lead. Darian will lose his ecclesiastical rights."

I shook my arm sleeve to them. "You must continue to wear the Papal Knights attire until you know it is safe to reveal your identity."

"What of you?" Trentham asked.

"I will go forth in my noble clothing. My wife will accompany me dressed as Lady Ana." I looked to Wensla. "It will be dangerous my love."

My beloved winked at me. "As I told you before, I am ready to die for you."

"That is suicide!" Trentham blurted out. "If the entire army pursues you and your bride, you are both guaranteed to be slain. There must be a better way."

"We will assist ya in this adventure," George said. He snarled his nose. His breath reeked of soured ale. "That ull even the odds."

"What would you have us do?" Edward asked.

I looked at these rugged deformed people. They stood eager to help us, yet they had never been formerly trained in battle. George was loud and fearless, but he was unskilled and uneducated. Cecil and Edward had not the bodies for combat. Leofrick was more of a clumsy jester than a respectable friar. Uther had the body of a warrior but the mind of a simple child. The rest of the misfits were common thieves who could do little more than a few tricks to scare the enemy. If I didn't include them, they might hinder our battle plan. I rubbed my chin. "If you stole the enemies' weapons and armor before they could use them…and…" I pursed my lips. "Perhaps you could also do some of your haunting with the nobility to frighten them away and afford us more time to run."

Vigilan and George looked at one another. Leo stared at me. Edward and Cecil threw up their hands and huffed. Sir Trentham shook his head.

"Adrian, may I speak with you alone?" Wensla

asked. I followed her outside the tent away from everyone. She sighed.

"What is the matter my love?" I asked.

"Remember what you told me about your feelings toward Marcus? You felt your chief knight disrespected you and your authority. You said he never was outright rebellious, but was very subtle in his disregard for you."

What point was Wensla trying to make? What did that have to do with my dealings with the misfits? "I recall that conversation," I said. "What are your intentions with this story?"

"Adrian." My beloved held my face in her hand. Her milk white skin was so cool and soft against my warm, rough face. "Tell me again how it made you feel whenever Marcus treated you as if you were less than he was."

"I felt like I had something to prove, as if I were less than a nobleman. I was angry toward Marcus and how he treated me. I had more to offer than what he or other..."

I stopped. A light brightened in my mind. I had treated the misfits the exact same way that Sir Marcus and the other noblemen in the kingdom had treated me. I remembered the vulgar comments from the high ranking rulers at the Great Hall meeting. I remembered all the petty words Sir Marcus spoke. It infuriated me against him. All of them were superior in skill to me, but I was not without merit and ability. Was this the way the misfits felt? Perhaps they did have much more to offer than I gave them credit for. I knew what I had to do. "I have been a fool," I said. "I must repent before God and before these misfits...I mean these people."

Wensla smiled and kissed me on the cheek. "That is the honorable man that I married."

We returned to the tent. Everyone nodded or shook their heads as they whispered to one another. The whispering stopped when they realized I was among them. All eyes fixed on me.

I cleared my throat. "George of Bahran, I have been less than chivalrous to you and your people. You are a great man who resides over wonderful servants. I wish to set things right between us and deliver the new battle plan, but I wish to do so with all those who reside in the land." I walked up to George and put my hand on his shoulder. "I humbly request that you assemble everyone together to hear my words."

George smiled his rotten grin. "Ya really mean good don't ya?"

I nodded. I meant every word I said.

George slapped me on the back. "I like the sound of that!" George removed the cat tooth necklace from his person and draped it around my neck. "This is Ghost's tooth. The crazy cat broke it off while nibblin on a piece of armor. He who wears this lords over eryone in Bahran. Give me some time, and I'll have the whole lot of them standin ready to hear yur ramblins!" He pounded his fist into his palm. "Edward and Cecil, fetch eryone right quick." George waved his pointing finger at the rest of us. "Foller me!"

We followed George toward the largest rocky wall in Bahran. He held a lit torch in his hand even though it was still light outside. It seemed as if we were going to march into the cliff itself. Just as we almost ran into it, the ground sank beneath our feet. The farther we walked, the lower it sank. It became a slope descending down into a cave. The cliff vanished from sight and an underground tunnel lay before us.

"Apparently we aren't the only ones with secret tunnels," Vigilan remarked. "Perhaps we could use these to reach The City unhindered."

"Yep," George replied. "Surely could."

We walked through a long corridor that howled with a warm wind. It led to an opening that looked like an arena. It was the same size as the coliseum that had crumbled from the olden days of The City. Marble seats lined each side of this massive hall and the ceiling reached higher than the tops of some castles. Passageways appeared in every place along the four walls. A raised platform containing several royal chairs sat in the middle of the arena floor.

George pointed toward the tunnels. "There is hot springs in some of these passages. That's why it's so warm year round. There are differn treasures in other passages. These caves lead to differn places all round the kingdom. That's the main way we move bout the differen lands." George pointed to a door embedded in one of the walls. "We can live down here durin an invasion or times of harsh frost."

"You have an arsenal?" Trentham pointed to weapons lined along the walls.

"That we do," George replied. "We train for combat here and do games. We not only learnt battle techniques of the knights, we learnt battle plans and skills from differn lands not known to yer people." He held out his arms as if welcoming someone. "This is our greatest secret in Bahran, and is only now I was sure we could trust ya with it."

"So the Drakes are not the only ones with powerful secrets," Eli remarked.

An underground travelling system? Their greatest secret? Treasures? Hot springs? Living quarters? War time training? Their level of trust in us had finally blossomed. My understanding and respect for them had blossomed as well. There was an entire world beneath our feet we never knew about. It seemed too good to be true.

"There they be!" George motioned for the misfits appearing through the various entrances. It looked like ants marching out of their dusty holes. Hundreds upon hundreds filled this grand assembly. It was larger than the gathering held in The City those many months ago. We ascended the steps leading to the platform and stood before the masses. They whispered and pointed to the necklace that dangled about my neck.

George showed Vigilan and the others to the royal chairs. He extended his hand toward the crowds while looking at me. "They are all yurs," he said. He made his way to his seat and crossed his arms.

Hundreds of deformed individuals waited for me to speak. I saw them in a different light. They were more than just the outcasts of society. They were gifted people that the world refused to accept. They were good people who had feelings, hopes, and desires like any other person. They were like me.

"Men and women of Bahran, I have humbly requested to meet with you this day," I began. "When

I first met you, I truly had no respect for your persons. I thought of you much in the same way as those you left behind in the towns. I was blinded to your beauty, your ability, and your intelligence. I had grown to admire your endurance in the face of such adversities. Some of your own had shown loyalty to my plight even when they had no obligation whatsoever to do so." I held my hands out. "For this cause, I humbly ask for your forgiveness."

Each word I spoke echoed in this vast arena. Except for an occasional cough or sneeze, the group remained totally silent and attentive to my words. I had never seen such respect given to someone, not even the pope himself. They looked to one another and nodded in unison to my plea.

"We are in great distress now. Our kingdom is in danger of being found and invaded, and I take full responsibility for this trouble I've brought upon you. I myself am an outcast of society who has been scorned by many. My accusers undermined my rank, my abilities, and my opinions." I pulled out my sword. "I ask all of you to kneel before me."

The entire assembly fell to one knee and bowed their heads. I stretched forth my sword and held it over the gathering.

"You have earned the right to have this honor bestowed upon you. I dub all of thee as knights in Bahran. You have obtained this honor just as I have. You have performed brave feats of chivalry that must be recognized. Now arise and receive the glory and responsibility of your new positions."

The masses of misfits rose to their feet and held up

their clenched fists. I raised my sword over my head. "For Bahran and for God!" I yelled

"For Bahran and for God!" the assembly cried.

I repeated those words over and over. I shook my sword each time I said it. My voice quivered and grew hoarse from yelling. The misfits matched my intensity with their voices. They stomped their feet. They clapped their hands. They jumped up and down. They raised their weapons.

We were ready. The time had come.

Chapter Twenty Two

W ensla and I set up a small camp along the main
highway leading to The City. I slept very little.
I stared into the night sky while listening for any commotion and watching for any movement. The misfits
planted rumors that I was on my way to the holy habitation with Lady Ana to expose an evil plot. These
same gossiping messengers informed me that a large
regiment was being assembled to hunt us down. The
forces consisted of knights from various kingdoms.
I gave our exact location in an attempt to lure my
enemies into a trap. The morning sun soon beamed
over the distant mountains. I prayed that everything
and everyone was in place.

"There he is!" a voice called from the distance.

Wensla and I mounted our horse and charged
across the countryside toward The City. Arrows
whizzed by and narrowly missed us. I raised my large
shield over our heads. The misfits had acquired this
enormous piece from savage barbarians who lived
on a remote island in the eastern sea. Several arrows
banged against our overhead covering and fell to the

ground on each side. Our horse was unaffected by the attack; the steed charged forward in powerful strides.

"Are you sure you want to go through with this my love?" I asked Wensla.

"I live for you and for God," she replied, "and I will die for you and for God."

The arrows stopped suddenly. I continued to hold the armament over our heads in case there were any stray shots forthcoming. My arm trembled from the weight of this cast iron piece overshadowing us. I saw a vast army appearing over the horizon. War horses mounted by skilled warriors and experienced knights bounded toward us in violent fury. It was frightening to see so many powerful fighters channeling their rage at someone such as me.

The Baron of Sansaat was one of the knights leading the charge. He laughed and pointed his sword in my direction. "Behold Sir Baby and his pagan mistress!"

I ignored the insults of this arrogant, boisterous man. I lowered the shield and pulled on the reins. The horse changed its course and galloped toward a nearby forest. I slowed my pace to allow the monstrous brigade to gain ground. Spears and javelins landed in the ground behind us.

"God be with us!" Wensla cried.

An arrow buzzed by and hit our steed in the side of its leg. It neighed loudly, hoisted its feet up into the air, fell backwards, and landed on Wensla and me. The buckler I had been holding served as a wedge between us. It felt like a castle wall had tumbled upon me. I saw the approaching hooves of many mares tearing up the earth beneath them as they moved closer and closer to where we were. I pushed against the shield with every bit of strength I had. It rose high enough for me to slide my legs out from underneath. I crouched down for more leverage.

"Hurry Wensla!" I cried. "I can't hold this for long and they will be upon us at any moment!"

"I can't make it!" Wensla pulled on her legs but they were stuck under the horse. "Leave me behind. It's you they are after."

"I live for you and for God," I said. "I die for you and for God."

The stallion and the shield suddenly became lighter. I fell down on the grass. Uther towered over us holding up the dead horse with his massive arms. Cecil pulled me to my feet and Edward pulled Wensla to hers. She limped badly.

"Hurry or they will make meat sticks of us!" Edward said.

The army had gotten so close; it caused the earth to tremble beneath us. My shoulder burned with pain, but I hobbled along with Wensla toward the forest. I was swept from my feet by an iron grip that constricted my chest. Uther had scooped me up with his right arm and ran toward the forest. Wensla was under his left arm. We bobbed up and down like bruised children in his vice-like hold.

"Follow them into the forest!" the Baron of Sansaat shouted in his gruff voice.

Uther took us inside a nearby large oak tree and closed the trunk. We watched through a peephole as several men entered the forest. They used their weapons to fold back plants. Some of them shouted curses at me. A large knight wearing black armor jabbed through holes in larger trees and waited for a reaction. When nothing happened, he moved on to other big trees and did the same.

"He's going to find us," Wensla whispered.

The knight in the black armor stopped in front of our tree and thrust his sword into one of the small slits in the bark. It missed us by only a hairbreadth. He jabbed his sword again into another part of the tree closer to where we were. The sword's point went toward my chest, but Uther moved his massive arm between the blade and my body. This giant child winced as blood trickled from his forearm. No one made a sound. The black armored warrior withdrew his sword and examined the steel. Even though his weapon had opened the giant's skin, no blood remained on the tip of the blade. The knight huffed and moved onward to another tree. I sighed in relief.

"Look!" I whispered. I pointed at two soldiers walking side by side. Leofrick followed behind them closely without making a sound.

"He will be caught," Wensla whispered. "There are knights all over these woods."

Leofrick tapped one of the men on the shoulder and dropped to the ground with his robe draped over his body. His cloak resembled a small mound of dirt sitting on the forest floor. The soldier looked behind him and then to his companion.

"What do you want?" he asked.

The other soldier shook his head. "What do you mean?"

"Why did you tap my shoulder?" the first soldier asked.

"I did no such thing," replied the other soldier. "Perhaps it was a spirit."

Leofrick came out of his ball like position and resumed to follow the men. He threw a stone and hit the other soldier on the back of the head.

The second soldier turned to the first. "Why did you strike me?"

"I did no such thing," replied the first soldier.

"Perhaps it was Bevol from the land of Carsen among the Hearsts," Leofrick said.

"Who said that?" the second soldier said.

I chuckled. Leofrick had used names that meant the wind from the marshlands dwelling among the woods.

Both soldiers looked behind them. Leofrick had wrapped himself once again into his mound shape on the ground.

"This forest is haunted!" Both men shouted to the others in unison.

Hands appeared out of the ground and pulled some of the knights into the earth. They shrieked in terror. A thick fog entered the forest and swirled around the ankles of the foot soldiers. They looked at one another and jerked in the direction of the slightest sounds.

"That cursed Adrian is being helped by demons!" a soldier cried out.

"That witch Ana must be conjuring them up for him!" another soldier added.

Rocks fell from the trees and crushed the heads of some of the knights. Ropes tripped some of the warriors and left them injured. All around the forest, scores of soldiers disappeared as misfits sneaked around and subdued them.

"Halt!" someone cried.

A Papal Knight rode into the forest on a white war horse. Two fingers were missing from his raised hand. "I have seen these brigands before, and they are a cunning foe. They want us to fight them on their own terms. If they were to engage us in the open field, we would slaughter the whole lot of them."

Who was this man that knew us? There were many Papal Knights that we encountered along the way. The knight removed his hood. It was Sir Marcus!

"What do you wish of us my lord?" one of the soldiers asked.

Marcus looked all around the forest. His face was scarred. His brazen colored hair had been sheared off. One of his ears was missing. My former chief knight looked half human and half monster. These injuries were probably due to the blow that the misfits delivered near Granes. "Adrian, you son of a jackal! I know you are in here!" Marcus shouted. He glanced around the forest once again as if he anticipated my appearance. "You cannot escape our hands! You and your rebellious friends will soon be sliced into small portions and fed to the fowls!"

"My lord?" the same soldier asked again.

"Burn this forest to the ground," Marcus growled. "We will drive them out of the forest to engage us in the open field. We will make quick work of them. If they so choose to remain here, these pagans will taste the flames of hell before they actually arrive there."

The knights nodded and quickly broke off low lying limbs from nearby trees. They gathered flint rocks and struck them together. Sparks flew into the sky and flames flickered on the branches. The soldiers dropped them along the ground and fled from the forest.

Marcus moved his horse toward the clearing and looked over his shoulder. "If the coward of Granes should dare face me, I promise to make his death a slow torturous affair. He will recount it through all eternity!" He snapped the reins and disappeared.

The flames spread along the ground and up the sides of the trees as smoke filled the forest. It burned my eyes and gagged me. Wensla and Uther coughed. Fire surrounded us as we sprang from the hollow oak tree.

"Try to extinguish those flames!" I ordered.

Wensla tore off the bottom portion of her skirt and swatted at the fires along the ground. The misfits took rags and anything else they could find to douse the blaze. Some of them tried to throw water out of their canteens to squelch the flames, but it spread faster than we could handle.

Edward bent over and blew at one of the burning embers. Each time he breathed on the fire, it flickered and grew larger.

"That is only making matters worse you ignorant slug!" Cecil shouted at Edward. He grabbed his brother by the ear and pulled him along.

George appeared through the rising smoke and pulled on my elbow. "We stay in here much longer, we're gonna be roasted like frogs in a boilin pot!"

He cupped his hands to his mouth. "To the fields and fight! All of ya!"

The misfits scrambled from behind every bush, from underneath rocks, from the tops of trees, and other places around the forest. They followed George toward the clearing like lambs going to a slaughter. I saw Marcus with his sword unsheathed in the clearing. He had dismounted from his steed. I knew he was waiting for me.

This was it. I was weary of his boastings. He had been a thorn in my side for a long time. I would no longer endure the ridicule from this pompous, vain troublemaker. I felt a surge of power rush through my limbs, and none of the pain that racked my body only moments before was affecting me. I unsheathed my sword in a furious rage and ran toward Marcus.

Chapter Twenty Three

"I've been waiting for this for a long time!" Marcus sneered.

My heart throbbed against my chest. I wasn't sure if I was more angry or nervous about engaging him. Was he still the same warrior or had the injuries inhibited his abilities? He raised his sword as I swung my blade. The swords rang into the air and sparks flew. I thrust my sword at him several times, but he dodged every attempt.

"Is that the best you can do?" Marcus mocked. "I know of milkmaids who handle a weapon better than you!"

"Be careful Adrian!" Wensla called out.

I caught a quick glimpse of my beloved. She wore a hood over her head and a veil across her face to conceal her identity.

"So you have the support of that witch Ana eh?" Marcus said. "When I am finished with you, I will cut her down as well. I will be the one to reign in Granes as I should have all along!"

"There is nothing chivalrous about you Marcus,"

I retorted. "You were a traitor to me long before this controversy." I swung my blade around and clashed against his raised sword. We pushed toward one another and stood nose to nose.

"You never could best me in sparring," Marcus bragged.

My muscles tightened as I pushed against him. He was much stronger than I, and he shoved me to the ground. He raised his sword over my head and aimed for my stomach as I lay before him.

"Marcus!" Wensla cried.

I rolled out of the way and leaped to my feet with my sword pointed toward my former chief knight. Marcus had jabbed into the ground where I had been. He yanked his sword from the dirt and shook it.

"I will pin you to the earth yet!" he scowled.

"You can try," I said.

"I would have removed you long ago if you weren't a necessary scapegoat for the plot. It was I who commanded your knights to kill those who spoke against you. It was I who sent a letter in your name giving that command." He pointed his blade in my direction. "You always were a weak ruler. I merely gave the orders you should have been strong enough to execute."

This rebel knight tricked my men into carrying out heinous crimes? So it was only he, not they, who had conspired against me. I gritted my teeth and lunged at him with my sword. He easily dodged and laughed.

"You are not deserving of the fair Wensla," Marcus said. He swiped his weapon at me. I nearly stumbled to the ground trying to dodge the strike.

"She would have hated me forever if I had harmed you. I knew that eventually she would realize that it would be better to be at my side than yours."

How dare this mangled troublemaker speak such things! The betrayal I had suspected all along was coming to light. I felt my face burning in anger, but I knew that I would be unfocused in this battle if I allowed my feelings to control me. I was sure this was Marcus' strategy.

"Come hither!" Marcus motioned for me with his deformed hand. "It is obvious that the truth bothers you. You know in your heart Wensla desires to be with me. You are like a little pigeon whose wing is broken. The kindness she has shown you over the years is out of pity."

Why was Marcus trying to lure me into a blind rage? Was he taunting me to add insult? Was he attempting to even the match by causing me to lose my temper? Whatever the reason and no matter what he said, I refused to let it trouble me. He wasn't aware that I was injured as well. If he wanted a war of words, I would engage him on this front also.

"The great Sir Marcus!" I held out my hands with my sword upraised. "It is you who should be pitied. You are locked up in your vanity while cheating and lying. You have broken every code of chivalry that there is. You call yourself a knight?"

Marcus didn't respond.

"Do you actually believe that the fair Wensla would care for the hideous beast you have become?" I smirked. "You know so little of either her or me."

"Even if he is a traitor, it is unbecoming of a

knight to slander the enemy," Wensla said to me from behind her veil. She stood near one of the trees outside the forest.

Wensla was right. I had lowered myself to use the same tactics as this treacherous fellow. There was no chivalry in my words. If I wished to be treated as a nobleman, I needed to act like one.

"You permit a reprobate woman to command you?" Marcus asked. "You are not even half the man I thought you were."

I looked around the battlefield. The misfits were outmaneuvering their foes and knocking them to the ground. The knights, the horsemen, and the other soldiers seemed terrified of these forces. Many of the misfits were decked out in their animal like armor. The ghostly army of Bahran shrieked and roared as if they were restless souls from another world. George growled from his gargoyle shaped armor and wielded his pike like one of the Crusaders. The spirit cat Ghost pounced on one soldier after another and ripped through them with its jagged claws. Uther smacked numerous knights across the field with large mallets he held in each hand. He caught horses in mid gallop, threw them up into the air, and slammed them into the ground. I pointed in all directions. "Look around you Marcus."

Marcus reacted to my request. For every one misfit that fell, three knights were defeated. Cecil and Edward tumbled along the ground like acrobats and bowled soldiers over onto the ground. Leofrick wound his slingshot and flung spoiled meat at the knights. The meat was thick enough to knock the enemy off of their horses.

"Your seasoned warriors are losing the fight against these lowly commoners," I said to Marcus. "There are more of us than there are of you now. You must surrender! You can't possibly take on all of us."

Marcus gritted his teeth and pointed his sword at me. "Even if it is with my dying breath, I will slay you and all these peasants who brought this curse upon me!" Marcus charged and swung his blade wildly. I held my weapon in a defensive stance and absorbed each blow. He struck so hard; I nearly lost my grip on the sword. He clashed against my sword over and over. Marcus' quickness prevented me from being able to counterattack. He continued to push forward while I continued to move backward. "I shall enjoy finishing you off!" he said.

This twisted knight tried to jab my skull. I didn't have time to position my sword and defend it, so I raised my other arm to block his weapon. The sword sunk into my skin. Warm, wet blood oozed from the wound. My forearm stung like burning fire as Marcus withdrew the weapon. I was stunned by this blow. I couldn't move. Marcus spun around and followed with a swiping blow to my left thigh. It tore my tunic open. Blood dripped from this wound as well. I fell to the ground and dropped my sword. "At last I will be rid of you!" Marcus turned his sword downward and held to it with both hands.

I knew what he was attempting to do. He was going to plunge the blade into my heart. If this were my fate, I would accept it. Dying on the battlefield was an honorable thing. It was better than living as a fugitive the rest of my days. I closed my eyes and prayed silently for God to receive my unworthy soul. I expected to feel the sharpened edge of Marcus' weapon sink into my chest at any moment, and then my breath would leave me.

"Wait Marcus!" I heard Wensla wail. "If you truly care for me, then you will not harm him."

I opened my eyes and saw Marcus standing over me with his sword positioned, but he was looking in Wensla's direction with surprise on his countenance. I turned and looked at Wensla. She had removed the hood and the veil. She ran toward Marcus and fell down at his feet sobbing.

"You!" Marcus' mouth flew open.

"It is the one you love," Wensla said through her tears. "I disguised myself to fool you and everyone into thinking I was Ana so we would be pursued."

Marcus did not move for several minutes. He looked like a statue standing over me. This deformed traitor acted as if he and Wensla were the only ones there. The battle raged on between the misfits and the knights in the distance. The forest looked like a fireball with smoke rising high into the heavens.

"Lady Wensla…I…" Marcus spoke much softer.

"You claimed you would not harm Adrian because you cared for me," Wensla said. She sniffled as tears streamed from her eyes. "I beg you for his life now, and I will be yours forever."

"You cannot do that Wensla!" I blurted out. I would rather die at the hands of this monster than be spared and live with the knowledge that Wensla would be in his clutches for the rest of her life. Papal

186

Knights were supposed to be holy men committed to chastity. Marcus had broken all the other vows; this one was apparently no different.

"I promise that I shall be yours if you will let Adrian live," Wensla repeated. She rose to her feet and placed her hand on his scarred face. "Please Marcus. Isn't that what you wanted all this time?"

I looked at Marcus' face. He was mesmerized by Wensla's beauty and her soft words. He dropped his arms and his sword dangled loosely in his hand. I lay there breathing heavy. The wounds Marcus inflicted on me throbbed badly. I tried to lift my arm to shoo Wensla away, but I didn't have the strength. I knew that if I wasn't treated soon, I would perish anyway.

"I will treat you well," Marcus whispered to Wensla.

Wensla tilted her head and kissed him. It was worse than if Marcus had ran me through the heart with his sword. I knew Wensla was trying to save my life, but did she have to kiss this ugly traitor? Perhaps it was punishment from God for what had happened between Ana and me on that moonlit night. I felt crushed inside. I renewed my vow never to betray my beloved again should we survive this ordeal. The mangled traitor dropped his sword and slid his arms around Wensla. The weapon hit my knee and fell on the ground beside me. Marcus suddenly stumbled backward and gagged. He clutched his stomach where a dagger protruded from it. Blood poured from his mouth, and he looked at Wensla in bewilderment.

"I'm sorry Marcus," she said.

I tripped Marcus as he lunged at my wife. He fell on his face and rolled around trying to remove the dagger. He yelled like an animal and spouted curses at Wensla and me. He squirmed for a few moments, and then he stopped moving.

George stood over me in his demon-like armor. He pulled his helmet off of his head, tossed it on the ground, and examined me. "Hard to fight a battle lyin on yer hind like that!" He laughed and breathed his rotten breath over me.

I wrinkled my nose and turned my head at the smell. He reached underneath me with both hands and pulled me to my feet by my armpits. I shivered from the blood loss. George whistled, and a misfit came with bandages. Wensla helped them wrap my wounds in the cloth.

"We beat these…these…" George scratched his head.

"Unwins!" Leofrick said as he waddled over to where we were.

"Unwins…enemies…uh…yes," George said. "Their carcasses are lyin all over the place. The rest of them ran away like swine runnin from a bath. I had to send Ghost home to Bahran with one of the other men. He was limpin round and lickin a bloody paw." He placed a hand on my shoulder. "The fight is done."

I looked down at the lifeless body of Marcus. I looked around at all the bodies strewn over the highway and the meadow. I watched the smoke billow from the nearby forest. I saw the misfits rejoicing over their hard fought victory. I looked at George and shook my head.

Chapter Twenty Three

"Not yet," I said. I pointed toward the highway leading to The City.

The final challenge awaited us there.

Chapter Twenty Four

Our small injured army marched slowly but proudly toward The City. Most of our forces brought no horses to battle, so they travelled on foot. I held a rope tied around a donkey's neck and steered it toward our destination. Wensla sat on that colt with her head bowed in silent prayer. A few survivors had escaped from our previous battle, so I assumed they would warn the larger forces that awaited us. The army of Papal Knights was the largest in the kingdom. I heard rumors that they were better trained than any other warrior in the entire realm. They fought with a religious zeal unknown to the typical knights. They were the kingdom's greatest fighters, but they were also the most merciful. I hoped to use this to our advantage.

"There they be!" George pointed at the horizon toward the entrance of The City.

I squinted and saw a sea of white robes in the distance. Their heads were tilted toward the heavens with their swords upraised. Their weapons glistened in the sinking afternoon sun. Pope Darian sat on a golden throne elevated above the army. The pope folded his hands in a gesture of prayer. His pupils were rolled back into his head until only the whites of his eyes could be seen. It seemed as if he were in a trance.

"They are not moving," Cecil said.

"That is obvious you dolt!" Edward said. "Why are they not moving?"

"They are playin cat and meese with us," George said. "They want us to waste our breath comin to them so we will be easy prey for em."

George was right. They sat still as statues even though we moved closer and closer. I expected them to break their stillness at any given moment and charge our small band. It was apparent that Eli, Leo, Vigilan, and Trentham had not been with the Council of Elders; otherwise this enormous brigade would not be there to crush us out of existence.

"Hold here," I commanded.

"You heerd em," George said. "Be put!"

The battered misfit army came to a halt. Our forces were in catapult's distance of the holy army. I released the rope of Wensla's donkey.

"Adrian, what are you doing?" Wensla asked.

"Wait here," I said. "Say a prayer for me."

I walked to the middle of the field between the opposing armies. Two Papal Knights appeared through the sea of white to meet me. I left my sword with Wensla so that I would not be mistaken for leading an attack. I held my hands up for them to see that I was defenseless. This meeting was my attempt to stall for time and avoid a massacre. The two Papal Knights who approached me bore no arms either.

I bowed my head. "Greetings in the Name of our Lord and Sav…"

"Spare us your vile welcome!" one of the Papal Knights spouted. "You will not utter the Name of God's holy Son!"

"His holiness has sent us forth with this message," the other Papal Knight said. "Surrender yourself and the harlot Ana or every one of your pitiful crusaders will be killed for their transgression."

Where were my friends? Had they been found and captured before reaching the council? Was there another traitor among us who had foiled the plan? I prayed not. I would not be able to stall these zealous mercenaries for too long. I wasn't sure how they would react once they found out that Lady Ana was really Lady Wensla. They were more than ready to slay me, and all those who were with me, in the Name of God.

"I wish to speak to Pope Darian," I said.

"The mouthpiece of God does not deal with reprobates!" the first Papal Knight growled.

"Will I be spared if I surrender?" I asked.

"You will be burned at the stake along with your demonic mistress," the second Papal Knight howled.

"Then what will become of the others who are with me?" I asked.

"If these pagans become Christians and renounce their former association with you, they will be spared and brought into our fold," the first messenger said.

"If they refuse to recant, they will be killed… every last one of them," the other messenger added.

The misfits had treated me well. I couldn't let

them or Wensla die at the hands of these misguided soldiers of light. If they only knew that their master was the real traitor. I believed these men, and most of the other members of the Papal army, were pure hearted servants of Christ. They were led to believe I was a heretic. They would not give audience to my accusations against the pope. I had to think of something else.

"Speak now!" the first knightly messenger snapped. "What say you to the Lord's representative on earth?"

I had to think fast. "Give this message to the one who sent you. Tell his excellency that I wish to repent of my wickedness and be absolved of all wrongdoing. I appeal to the mercies of God and that of the church."

The Papal Knights looked at one another and nodded without saying another word. They made their way back into the mass of white knights. The sun was setting by this time and made a fiery red glow against the backdrop of the gates to the holy capital. My armpits were drenched in sweat. Would they accept this feeble plea for mercy? Even though I had been excommunicated, clergy often showed pity to those who cried out for forgiveness. The two messenger knights were gone for a long time. I stood there with the eyes of both armies watching my every movement.

I dropped to my knees and raised my arms. "I ask for mercy and a hearing before God and all of you." My arm and leg stung from the wounds Marcus inflicted upon me. Surely my pitiful appearance in these bandages would draw sympathy from such noble and holy men.

No one moved. No one smiled. Intense glares from the soldiers on the front line bore holes through me. Zeal blazed in their eyes. If this plan didn't work, I would surrender to spare the lives of my friends and suffer whatever fate the Lord allowed.

"Make way for the Shepherd of shepherds!" the two Papal messengers called out in unison.

Soldiers parted like a giant sea of white to allow the pope to come forward. A powerful presence surrounded Darian as if unseen forces walked beside him. Cold chills ran through my body. I felt something dark emanating from his person.

"So the heretic who has brought so much trouble to our kingdoms wishes to plea for his life?" Darian asked. His deep voice seemed to shake the nearby flowers. "It is an attempt to trick us and cause more destruction."

"It is you who has tricked the people and tried to bring ruin upon our kingdoms!" I shouted at the pope. "God did not place you over His sheep. You have taken them through cunning lies and tried to silence those who spoke otherwise!"

The two Papal Knights who accompanied Darian raised their hands to strike me for insulting their leader. I held my hands up in submission. It was foolish to have taken such an approach. Darian motioned for the knights to lower their arms.

"Beelzebub possesses your blackened spirit." Darian shook his head. "It is apparent that your soul is already lost. You have gone beyond the possibility of forgiveness in this world and the world to come."

"I have been accused of things that I had no part of," I said in soft tones. "I have proof of my innocence and your guilt."

"Where is this proof?" Darian demanded. "Show us."

I dropped my head. Without the Drake scrolls, the confessions of the various traitors, and the other pieces of evidence, I had no way to prove my claims. What were my words against the word of the highest member of the church and all of the supposed proof against me? I had made no impression on these knights. I had to think of another strategy. "I wish to have the peace and love of God in my heart again." I shook my head. "I am truly sorry for my sins. I have mistreated people for so long." Tears welled up in my eyes. "I have suffered much, but in Christ there is pardon."

"That would only be for the truly penitent," Darian snorted. "You speak these things out of a desire to save your neck and not from a contrite heart."

"How do you know of my sincerity?" I asked. I was repentant, but it was over the ways I had betrayed Wensla, my mistrust of Leo, and how I had treated the misfits. It had nothing to do with the false charges this deviant church head had brought against me.

Darian's eyes widened. He made the symbol of the cross with his fingers. "Demons have driven you to madness! One moment you spew lies against the Lord's anointed, and the next moment you grovel for pity on your condemned soul."

"Is there no justice among you?" I cried out to the white knights that stood behind him. "Seek out the truth dear brothers. You are about to strike down an innocent man."

Darian made his way back to his throne. "Da, quaesumus Dominus, ut in hora mortis nostrae Sacramentis refecti et culpis omnibus expiati, in sinum misericordiae tuae laeti suscipi mereamur. Per Christum Dominum nostrum. Amen." Darian poised himself in his seat and continued to chant the prayer. He stared into the distance as if peering into the spirit world.

I recognized the Latin words Darian uttered. It was a prayer for a happy death. I had no other schemes to prolong this execution. No one listened to me and no one believed me. I had no other choice now. I had to surrender myself to save the others. I raised my hands in submission. "I turn myself over to your hands. Please spare the others who are with me."

The pope ignored my proposal. It was obvious that he intended to have us all slain. Darian raised his finger as he chanted several other prayers. The Papal Knights closed their left fists and smote their breasts. They swung their right arms over the top of their left arms and formed a cross over their hearts. They clutched firmly to the swords in their right hands.

"In nomine Patris, et Filii, et Spiritus Sancti. Amen."

They chanted over and over. The cries began softly but grew louder with each passing moment. These knights of the light sang the words in perfect harmony. It sounded like an angelic choir. Their musical tones rang throughout the countryside. In spite of the eminent danger, the melody of those elegant voices formed waves of peace inside the deep of my heart. It was unlike any war call I had ever known. I heard Leo's voice calling in the deep of my heart.

Trust no one but God.

I knew what I had to do. Unseen celestial hands guided me as I slowly made my way back to my small army. Wensla seemed to be mesmerized by the holy war chant while the misfits appeared to be entertained. I turned to face the singing army and dropped to my knees.

"Kneel with me before the Lord and bow your heads," I ordered.

Wensla and the misfits looked at me with stunned expressions.

"Kneel with me before the Lord and bow your heads!" I repeated with more authority. We had only moments to spare.

Wensla and all of the misfits complied with my command.

"Dear Father in heaven," I began. I looked toward the sky and extended my hands upward. The wondrous voices drove me to prayer. "I do not know all the Latin words, but I ask Thee in these waning hours of my life to accept this plea in my own tongue."

The singing of the warrior monks continued. It became so loud that I could not hear my own voice as I spoke.

"O my God, I love Thee above all things, with my whole heart and soul, because Thou art all good and worthy of all love." I cried out as loudly as I could. "I love my neighbor as myself for the love of Thee. I forgive all who have injured me, and ask pardon of all whom I have injured. Amen."

"Amen." Wensla and the misfits repeated.

Darian dropped his finger, and the Papal Knights' singing became cries of war. They charged toward us with great fury. I closed my eyes, held fast to Wensla, and awaited the zealous attack.

Chapter Twenty Five

The hoof beats of war horses thundered all around me. Wensla huddled close and squeezed my arm. I kept my eyes closed. Several minutes passed, yet nothing pricked me. I looked up and saw wisps of light flowing around our entire army. My mouth flew open. Wensla, George, and the rest of the misfits gasped at the sight. The Papal Knights surrounded our camp on all sides, but they could not pass through the shimmers of light.

"What sort of magic is this?" one of the holy knights asked. He tried to force his way through but was knocked backward to the ground.

"Your holiness, demons are blocking our way!" another Papal Knight cried out.

We rose to our feet and watched the light show. I reached out to touch one of the glowing beams. A soft, cool breeze rolled through my inner being. The hair on my arms stood up as peace filled my mind. I felt waves of strength surging into my injured body.

George poked the light and looked at his finger. "Looks like we took friends to a swarm of fireflies!"

"Perhaps this is the hand of the Lord," a Papal Knight said.

"Christ would not protect such sinners as these," another holy soldier remarked.

"Do not be fooled by the wiles of the devil," Darian cried. "The fallen angel of light fights for these wretched souls! It is a false shining." Darian clenched his fist and shook it at me. "God shall overcome you, spawn of Satan!"

"Are not demons from the darkness?" another white knight asked. "This is a miracle of the light."

"You dare challenge my authority?" Darian roared.

"No your glory," another knight said. "Forgive us for trying to interpret matters of the church apart from your divine guidance."

"The wicked Lady Ana is the source of this witchery." Darian pointed toward Wensla. "Once she is smitten, they will be powerless to defend themselves."

Wensla removed her hood and dropped the veil from over her face. "We have tricked you. I am Lady Wensla of Granes. Ana is hidden far away from here."

Darian raised his eyebrow. "So you have conspired together with that sorceress?"

"We have not conspired with anyone," I said. I pointed in the direction of the pope. "It is you who have conspired against the kingdom of God. You have tried to silence me and all those who stand for Leo."

"Blasphemous lies from condemned souls," Darian snorted. "The fallen one has so possessed your minds that none of your speech bears any truth."

"Buckminster speaks no lies," Leofrick said. He dusted grass off of his robe. "His mouth has been purified with soured goat's milk mixed with cattle dung." He rubbed his chin. "Perhaps you should consider this cleansing."

"These vermin are not only liars, they are insane," a Papal Knight said. He signed the cross.

"Lady Ana found Adrian in Granes holding the ancient parchments of the Drakes," Wensla said. "She used these tricks to deceive the masses. She gloated over how her secret followers, along with other lords and kings, plotted to bring you into the papacy and eliminate any who opposed you."

"We banished the Drakes many generations ago," one of the Papal Knights said.

"They were our sworn enemies," another knight remarked.

The white robed soldiers examined Darian as if seeing him from another perspective for the first time. Some rubbed their chins and mused the situation. Color drained from the face of the pope, but his countenance remained unchanged.

"Demonic illusions dreamed up in your depraved minds." Darian laughed with a calloused tone. "You have no proof. It has been proven, however, that you tried to maul innocent people throughout the kingdom, and that many have witnessed the terror you and your friends have caused. You would say anything to preserve your miserable lives!"

The Papal Knights nodded to the pope's answer and watched us with renewed vengeance in their eyes. Many of their faces burned red with anger.

They spouted taunts at me, Wensla, and the misfits. A twisted smile broke across the face of the reigning pope. Darian had the upper hand. It was the word of the most revered figure in the entire world against the word of lowly fugitives. The false evidence against me gave further credence to the pope's accusations. It was obvious who would be believed.

The holy army circled our battered group many times. They examined the swirling light barrier and looked for an opening they could enter into. The sun vanished and the twinkling stars shone overhead. The shield of light kept everything bright during the evening and early morning hours. No one spoke during this time and no one slept. Other than an occasional neighing from one of the mares or a grunt from the members of each army, there was no noise at all. The dawn of a new day soon broke over the nearby hillside. This miracle was the only thing that had kept me and my friends from certain and instant martyrdom. Perhaps this was the key to declaring my innocence. I decided to break the long period of silence.

I twirled around in a circle with my hands outstretched. "Behold this display of power that keeps us from your mighty hands!" My wounds stung afresh from my sudden movements. "Tell me." I rubbed my palms up and down against the bright wall. It formed small waves which grew larger as they moved outward as if I had dipped my hand into a stream. "Is not the Lord Jesus Christ greater than the forces of hell?"

Everyone snapped to attention at this sudden outburst and focused on me.

"Your tongue is black with the venom of heretical

words," Darian said. He held his hand in the air as if swearing an oath. "Christ is greater than all."

"I believe so too," I said. "Why is it that you, as servants of the Most High, have not conquered this wall and slaughtered us already?" I put my finger into my chest. "After all, you claim we are the offspring of the evil one."

Darian clenched his fists and gritted his teeth. His face became red as blood. For the first time in our exchange, he had nothing to say. The knights looked to one another once again. Wensla and the misfits nodded their approval of my words.

"Is it I who speak lies?" I placed my hand over my heart and then extended the same hand toward the pope. "Or is it you?"

Darian made no reply. He folded his hands to pray and resumed his Latin chanting. Deep groans resonated from his voice. Was this his attempt to answer my challenge?

"Adrian, look!" Wensla pointed to the glowing wall. It was fading from sight.

"Prepare for battle!" I raised my sword high over my head to signal the ailing misfit army as our last bit of protection disappeared. I refused to believe God favored Pope Darian and was answering his meditations.

The Papal Knights pulled on their reins and steadied their horses. They raised their weapons and poised to strike as the bright shield slowly vanished. Darian raised his forefinger once again. The last traces of the shining barrier faded away.

"Stay your ground!"

A group of decorated horses rode in between the army of holy knights and our forces. It was Eli, Leo, and the Council of Elders from The City. They were arrayed in scarlet robes and carried golden crosses in their hands. The Papal Knights stood motionless and waited.

"The only prayer you should utter is the Actus Contritionis!" Leo said to Darian.

"What is the meaning of this outrage?" Darian demanded. He rose to his feet and clapped his hands. "It is I alone who hold the keys of Peter!" He pointed to Leo. "Arrest this blasphemer and remove him from the earth!"

"The Shepherd of God does not harm the sheep!" one of the council members said. He held a scroll high and waved it before all. "These letters have the signature of Darian. He is in league with the Drakes. He is also involved in an immoral affair with their leader."

"Impossible!" Darian roared. "Has the council gone mad as well?"

"Furthermore, here are the parchments of the Drakes. It contains secret arts they have used to spread chaos throughout the kingdom." A wrinkled, silver haired elder waved another scroll. "Our servants have confirmed their presence in Granes after Adrian was banished."

Beads of sweat appeared on Darian's forehead. "My dear brothers, it is obvious that the forces of hell are conspiring to overthrow me. Surely you have enough spiritual insight to see this."

"The only conspiracy is that which was orchestrated by you!"

Vigilan and Sir Trentham emerged over the horizon with other knights from Tiempo. Vigilan threw a helmet onto the ground. I recognized the armor. It belonged to one of the knights who had engaged us in the forest and had fled from the battle.

"This helmet belongs to one of many rebels we found fleeing along the highway," Trentham said. "We took them captive."

Vigilan pointed toward the armor piece. "If you examine the markings along the side, you will see that it is from the county of Sansaat. Their baron was the biggest supporter of Darian during the election."

"These knights confessed to being in league with Pope Darian," Trentham said. "Their lords and bishops received large ransoms from church coffers. We discovered many privileges granted in letters signed by the pope himself."

The Church Council whispered to one another. The wrinkled, silver haired elder cleared his throat. "Based on this evidence, the church must…"

"Where is Darian?" Vigilan interrupted.

The pope was nowhere to be found. He had eluded everyone while Trentham and Vigilan had been talking. Heads turned all around and murmurings filled the air as hoof beats pounded the ground from a single horse. Pope Darian raced past everyone with a cloud of thick, black smoke trailing behind him. Everyone who fell into the path of the dark mist coughed and gagged. Some stood frozen as if taken by surprise by the pope's sudden escape. Others ran to the aid of those who were choking.

"Some…one stop…Darian!" Vigilan put his hand

to his mouth and coughed. His eyes were closed and tears flowed from the heaving.

The pope's steed was in full stride. He moved farther and farther into the distance. I thought of all the trouble this man had brought upon the kingdom. I saw the faces of all those who suffered in Granes. I thought of the grief Wensla experienced. Holy rage flared from the depths of my being. I twisted my body around and flung my sword as if I were carried by an unseen force.

"For the sake of Christ and all Christendom!" I shouted.

The sword twirled round and round until it came down and struck Darian in the back. He fell from the horse and it galloped away. Sharp pain riddled my body and the world seemed to spin. Then everything grew black.

Chapter Twenty Six

"Awaken my love."

The bright light blinded me. Wensla sat over me dabbing a rag on my brow. The cool, damp cloth chilled me as a trickle of water moved down my face. I was lying in a bed.

"What happened?" I whispered.

Wensla kissed my brow. "You fainted after losing so much blood. The physicians worked with you day and night. Leo and Eli have fasted and prayed for you ever since you fell ill."

I turned my head to the right and the left. I saw the familiar furniture of my bedroom. Beams of sunlight shone through the window and warmed my face. "Are we…"

"We're home," Wensla said. "Many townspeople have stopped by to offer their sympathies and their apologies for mistrusting you."

I looked toward the ceiling. Was this a dream? Were those months of hiding, running, fighting, and scavenging really over? I had to know more. "Wensla?" I rolled over to my side. Burning pain racked my body as I turned.

"Don't move so suddenly my love." Wensla patted my arm. "You have been lying there for a week now."

It only seemed like it was moments ago that I was on the battlefield staring at Pope Darian and the army of Papal Knights. I felt my face. Stubble scratched the palms of my hands. "What happened during my faint?"

"Many things." Wensla looked out the window and pursed her lips. "After you fainted, Sir Trentham carried your body to Tiempo at the command of my father. You were there for three days while the physicians treated your wounds and kept your body warm. Eli sat over you chanting many prayers. Once we realized you would live, I ordered that you be returned to Granes with me."

I nodded and smiled. "I must thank each of them for their loyalty and help." I closed my eyes. "What is happening around the kingdom?"

"My father returned to his kingdom, and Eli is the abbot of Dayma once again." Wensla unfolded a blue linen sheet and draped it across my feet and legs. "The blow you struck Darian with was fatal."

I pulled myself up and leaned on my elbows with every bit of strength I could muster. I trembled in this position, but I didn't care. This was a momentous occasion. "Then that means…"

"The conspiracy against Christendom is no more. Lady Ana and the other Drakes have been imprisoned and will be executed. The other conspirators throughout the kingdom have been arrested and await trial." Wensla motioned her hands downward as if to calm me and keep me from rising too suddenly. "The Council of Elders renounced the charges against all of us. Leo is to be christened as the new pope."

"When will this happen?" I wanted to be present when Leo ascended to the papacy.

"It will be announced soon." Wensla sighed and dropped her head.

"What is it my fair one?" I saw concern in her blue eyes.

"All church privileges have been restored to everyone but you. Our marriage has not been reinstated yet."

"Why would they do this?" I asked. "Did they not discover my innocence in all the charges?"

Wensla took my hand and rubbed it. "Eli thinks it has something to do with your slaying the pope. Even though he was a wicked man, he was still the Lord's anointed. It is the same as when David refused to lift his hand against King Saul in ancient Israel."

I sighed and slid back down into bed. It never occurred to me that I would be sinning by slaying the pope. I did so with the purest of intentions. I felt no condemnation in my heart. If God did not require this of me, would His servants do so?

Someone knocked on the door to the bed chamber.

"Enter," I said.

One of the manor servants came into the room holding a parchment. His eyes widened and his mouth opened. "Lord Adrian? Are you well?"

"I am fine," I replied. "What news do you bear?"

The servant unraveled the scroll and cleared his throat. "The household of Granes has been summoned to appear at The City three days from now." He quickly rolled up the parchment and shook it. "I will tell everyone the good news of your recovery." He disappeared in a flash.

Wensla and I looked to one another. Perhaps I would once again be pleading my case before the Head of the Church. This time, I was more confident in my chances.

Three days later, I entered The City with Wensla and my fellowship. The flag of Granes waved proudly in the wind. Everyone we met along the way gave looks of surprise and offered words of comfort. Lords, ladies, clergymen, and peasants alike watched me intently and whispered to one another. Was I the scourge of the kingdom once more, or were they merely amazed at my recovery? My clan took its place in the Great Hall. Vigilan stood on the other side with the house of Tiempo. He nodded to me and smiled. I watched the Council of Elders anoint Leo, commission him, and announce his papacy. The hall erupted with clapping and shouts of admiration. I was one of them. Although I was still weak from my recent wounds, I cheered with every ounce of strength I had. A man ridiculed and scorned by the kingdom stood proudly wearing the hat and robes of the highest office in the church. Of all the popes I had known in my lifetime, he deserved the honor more than any other. After several minutes of celebration, Pope Leo turned to the assembly and held out his hands to silence the throng.

"Dear children, we have all suffered much under Satan's oppression," Leo began. "A new day has dawned under the direction of God Himself. I am humbled by this great honor to stand before you as God's representative on earth." Tears welled in his eyes and coursed down his cheeks. "It is not by might that we lead, but by His Spirit." He raised his right hand to Heaven and lifted his face toward the sky. "As God Almighty lives upon His throne, so shall I be an instrument of righteousness in His hands for the care of all His sheep."

Applause began again for this wise man. He wiped the tears from his eyes while the clapping continued. He nodded and acknowledged the admiration of those assembled. After a few minutes, the cheering subsided again.

"There is unfinished work to be done," Pope Leo said. He extended the staff that was in his left hand toward the crowd. "George of Bahran and Adrian of Granes, come forward."

George appeared through the crowds of people lined up on the other side of the hall. Edward, Cecil, Leofrick, Uther, and many of the other misfits were with him. They were adorned in newly woven royal attire. I stepped out and walked toward the steps leading to the papal throne. Leo, the council, and the gathered masses examined me in hushed silence. George and I walked side by side, ascended the steps, knelt before Pope Leo, and kissed his ring.

"George of Bahran," Leo said. "You have lived in exile and watched over these outcasts of society. Your methods were at times questionable, but I have seen that your motives were pure. You loved the unlovable and cared for those for whom no one cared. For this, I commend you before God."

George smiled his snaggled smile and nodded.

Leo took a scroll from the hand of a nearby Papal Knight and unfolded it. "Rise before me, George of Bahran."

George stood up and faced the pope.

"The former lord of the county Sansaat was a traitor to his people. Those who lived there were massacred at his hands. The land is beautiful and quite bountiful. The king wishes to bestow this to your keep and make you the baron. Do you accept this offer?"

"Do we still be keepers of Bahran?" George asked. "Some of my friends wanna be put where they are, and some wanna be in a new home."

"Of course," Leo replied. He leaned toward George's ear. "All of its secrets shall remain with you as well," the elder pope whispered.

George turned and looked to the misfits. They speedily nodded their approval. George looked at the king who stood nearby. The black haired ruler with his thick black mustache nodded his consent. George looked at Leo and patted his chest. "We be honored your whiteness!"

I knew that all of those who knew the secrets of Bahran would remain silent. The misfits had learned to trust us, and we were honor bound to abide by that trust.

"Done." Leo clapped his hands together. "The two kingdoms shall be made into one." Leo took a horn of oil and poured it on George's head. "By the authority of the king of the land and that of the pope, you have hereby been granted lordship over the county of Sansaat and the land of Bahran. May you serve its people well."

George bowed before Leo then turned to the king and bowed before him. Oil dripped off the tips of his tangled hair.

"Adrian."

I looked into Leo's face. His countenance was stern. He did not use my designation of lord, nor did he announce my county of origin. I bowed my head before this great man.

"You smote and killed God's representative on earth."

My eyes were closed. I awaited punishment, banishment, or possibly execution. I knew Pope Leo was only doing what he was called to do. I had resolved to accept whatever he deemed appropriate.

"As the sword left your hands, I saw an angelic figure guide the blade and force it into the body of Pope Darian. No mortal could throw a sword to such a distance. It was the judgment of God upon him. Your faith in Christ permitted the angels of the Lord to protect you and your friends long enough to allow time for the Council of Elders to be called upon and for the other rebels to confess to the conspiracy." Leo tapped my head. "Rise before me Adrian of Elos."

"Elos?" I asked. My hands and knees shook as I rose in his presence. Would I be lord over several counties, two of which were Granes and Tiempo? Being Earl of Elos was to be the most powerful ruler in the entire realm outside of the king himself.

"The Earl of Elos was another who took part in the conspiracy against the kingdom. It was he who appointed Lady Ana in your stead at the whim of Pope Darian. The king suggested that you claim this position."

I turned to the king. He smiled and nodded his approval. I touched the sides of my head and extended my hands toward him in a gesture of gratitude.

Leo extended his staff and tapped me on the shoulder. "Adrian of Elos, you have restored the fortunes of many, including my own. By your leadership, the darkness of sin has been exposed and removed from the land." Leo looked in the direction of the misfits. "You have also brought those who were formerly outcasts into a home where they will be honored and well cared for." Leo turned to all those in the Hall. "What is from within proves the worth of a man. We have learned the true meaning of God's words. Man looks upon the outward appearance, but God looks upon the heart. This day, let everyone of us see all men as God sees them."

"Amen," the Hall said in unison.

Leo turned to me. "All church privileges, including your marriage to Lady Wensla, have been restored to you."

I turned and looked at Wensla. She smiled at me with those ruby red lips. I bowed my head before the elder pope to receive this commission.

Leo took another flask of oil and poured it over my scalp. "By the authority of the king and that of the church, I dub thee Earl of Elos." The warm ointment oozed around my ear lobe and dripped down my neck.

Chapter Twenty Six

"Earl Adrian and Lord George, face the assembly."

George and I stood erect and turned to the crowd.

"May I present Adrian, Earl of Elos and George, Baron of Sansaat-Bahran."

The assembly erupted in cheers. The nightmare was over. I finally understood what Leo, Wensla, and Eli were talking about. I learned to see myself and others the way God sees us. It was inner strength that proved the true worth of someone. The misfits in the kingdom became living proof of that. Glorious days and blessings lay ahead for us all.

CPSIA information can be obtained
at www.ICGtesting.com
Printed in the USA
LVOW11s1340270317
528621LV00001B/5/P